Charles Heathcote has a
very rarely leaves. A Crea
Cheshire and secretary
Writing Group, he is a w
Doris Ahoy is the third
featuring Mrs Doris Copeland.

...onologues

#1

Also Available

Our Doris
Indisputably Doris

DORIS AHOY

Charles Heathcote

VA

VARIOUS ALTITUDES

Cheshire

www.variousaltitudes.com

ONE

Our Doris gets some sort of malicious glee out of making me wear a tie to breakfast. All the other husbands get away with polo shirts. Cyril Marsden even got away with pyjamas when his Betty ate a bad scallop in Sardinia. I, however, have to wear a shirt and tie. Our Doris has my outfits planned out for the entire cruise, right down to my socks. It doesn't matter that we'll never see our fellow passengers again once the cruise is over, our Doris says we must strive to leave a lasting impression.

'Lasting?' I said, 'From the look of them, they won't be lasting much longer. The undertakers may as well be waiting at the dock, coffins in tow.'

Our Doris gave me the Look and said to me, she said, 'With that attitude, I might phone ahead with your measurements.'

I kept quiet after that. It's not that I'm scared of our Doris, I just worry about what she could do when we're miles from the mainland, on international waters with nowhere to run.

We were in our cabin at the time. Our Doris had me fork out extra so she could stay above deck – she has this belief that should we go the same way as the Titanic we'll get priority boarding for the lifeboats.

It's an all right cabin if I'm being honest. There's something of a balcony and enough space that it doesn't feel like we're dining first class in Alcatraz.

Our Doris isn't the biggest fan of the décor but then she's never gone in for neutral tones. It doesn't matter if it's fashionable, she's not interested unless it has a floral print. She stopped watching Homes Under the Hammer when they started decorating everything in beige. I remember her storming over to turn the television off at the wall and saying, 'Never before has there been a more vomit-inducing colour than beige.'

I said, 'You wear beige all the time, our Doris.'

She glowered. 'Yes I do, our 'arold, but that's because I am blessed with the knowledge of how to properly accessorise.' After this she spent days corresponding with an assortment of editors at various home design magazines expressing her distress at the utter lack of colour in modern decorating styles throughout the British Isles.

She received no replies.

I said to her, I said, 'Beige is the way it's done nowadays, our Doris.'

She said nothing and cancelled her subscription to Ideal Home.

Still, I think she's forgiven the ship its beige. They've supplied her with a desk, and it's got her acting all Theresa May as she keeps up with her correspondence. At first, I wondered just who she could be sending letters to and then I realised my wife will write to anyone she feels in need of a note. She once wrote a letter to a Waitrose cashier remarking on her heavy make-up, much too dark a shade for her skin tone, and failure to offer the rudimentary free cup of coffee.

Since we have arrived our Doris has written notes to everyone from the maid – who did not vacuum thoroughly enough, and our Doris found a few crumbs of indeterminate origin behind the bedside cabinet – to one of the chefs in the hopes they would give her their recipe for Scandinavian meatballs. Yet the woman she writes to most of all, who has become the talking point of our bedtime conversations is Mrs Veronica Ambrose.

I suppose our Doris's fascination with her all started when she found out about the community noticeboard. Our Doris loves a notice. When the Gazette arrives back home, the first thing she does is check the obituaries – once you pass seventy-one it's the only notice your friends put out.

We'd barely unpacked our suitcases when she discovered the community noticeboard. At least she claimed she read about it in the new cruiser's handbook but knowing my wife she will have read all about it six months beforehand, concocted some scheme on how to best use the community noticeboard and planned on making the community noticeboard the highlight of our trip.

She said to me, she said, 'I like to take an interest in the activities of my peers. It's all part of what makes me such a skilled hostess.'

'A snoop more like,' I said.

She gave me the Look and said, 'Come now, 'arold, isn't this all part of the adventure?'

I must admit she had me there. This trip is all about the two of us being free of Partridge Mews rumours and gossip. We haven't holidayed in years, not since the Torquay debacle of two thousand and three that resulted in the loss of three pairs of socks, an entire picnic, including Thermos, and the disappearance of our Doris's hat.

And now we're on the ocean.

It's not quite an M6 service station but it's nice enough.

I looked at our Doris all gone out. I'd anticipated finding our cabin, taking off my shoes and sleeping until dinner. Now I had to traipse around the various corridors, nooks and crannies like searching for a lady of the night in a blackout.

After fifteen minutes of walking my feet ached. I swear our Doris buys my shoes two sizes too small to stop me running away.

She's bought my shoes since nineteen seventy-two when I made the mistake of wearing sandals in Blackpool. She said as they had no place on a middle-class foot and that there's nothing more common than having your big toes on display.

My shoes have felt too tight ever since; a constant reminder of my minor indiscretion. As we wandered around the corridors, our nostrils stinging after someone went wild with the pine disinfectant, my toes felt as though they were eroding further with each step.

It didn't help when we spent half an hour circling the dining hall before realising why we'd developed a craving for quiche.

I said to our Doris, I said, 'I don't think I can go on much longer, my feet feel like bricks.'

She offered this smile, not the one she uses when she's about to spit venom in your eye, just the one that makes you realise she's clearly descended from

Godzilla, and she said to me, she said, 'At your age one can expect some pain commonly associated with arthritis, but it must be remembered that it is best to keep moving. Otherwise, you run the risk of becoming sedentary, growing obese, and I refuse to have an obese husband, our 'arold. Suppose it got around that I allowed my husband to over-indulge? That I did not make sure he lived a healthy lifestyle as befits the modern age – I cannot believe you would suggest such a thing. Has fifty-six years taught you nothing?'

I kept quiet after that.

It had been a while since our Doris ranted about anything. It were almost pleasant to go weak at the knees for something other than a prostate exam.

It took us the best part of an hour to discover the community noticeboard. Turns out we went the wrong way as soon as we left the cabin. I shouldn't be surprised. Our Doris has always been a fan of the scenic route, when she were in labour with our Angela she had me drive past the Sterling's farm so she could see the lambs.

The community noticeboard hung on a wall at the end of a corridor that dim I wondered that we hadn't set foot in a horror film, just waiting for Christopher Lee to come along and slaughter us as we tried to figure out what Herbert in room thirty-seven meant by NSA fun.

Apart from Herbert thinking himself the ocean's answer to Don Juan there were notices advertising Pilates, an early morning ramblers meeting, the recipe for a cauliflower cheese soup approved by Weight Watchers – probably because no one wanted to flaming eat it – and an invitation to a prestigious new club, run by none other than Mrs Veronica Ambrose.

The Hat Club, she'd called it – an invitation to the women on the ship to come together and get to know one another.

Our Doris weren't happy.

I could tell that she weren't happy.

She looked as though she were passing a gallstone.

I said to her, I said, 'What's the matter, our Doris?'

She showed me her notice and I understood just what had upset her. Her brow crinkled that much it looked as though the shark from Jaws had manifested on her forehead. She said to me, she said, 'Can you believe it, our 'arold? I've been planning this since we first got the brochure only to find I've been pipped to the post.'

And then she said something I never thought our Doris would say. She crumpled the note in her handbag and said, 'I don't know why I bother.'

Our Doris looked dejected, like a grape forgotten at the bottom of the fruit bowl. I would've put my arm around her had she not always warned me against public displays of affection.

Apparently, the need to flaunt your love in front of people is not in keeping with British standards, entirely European and can lead to severe depression for those unable to make a lasting connection with another human being.

At least that's what she told me on our wedding night. That's when most of the troubles started was our wedding night. No sooner had she declared herself Mrs Doris Copeland than she was transformed from loving fiancé into a domineering force of nature willing to withhold meals so as I would paint the back bedroom. She said as that's what made her a devoted housewife. I said as that could make her a divorced housewife.

In retaliation she wrote a letter to the Partridge Mews Gazette informing them that she accidentally married a misogynist who refused to help with household duties, pestered her for sex and expected his tea on the table by six.

Naturally, other wives in town sent letters of support, and the following weekend I found myself and the lads from work redecorating the entire house from top to bottom for nothing more than three pots of stewed tea and a plate of potted beef sandwiches. She even had Ira Murgatroyd donkey-stone the front step.

Now, because of that and a whole host of misdemeanours in the last fifty-six years, we were stood in the corridor on a high-end cruise ship and I couldn't even put an arm around my own wife to console her. Instead, I went with the only thing that had helped me with similar situations in the past. I said to her, I said, 'Let's go for a coffee, our Doris.'

We went to the coffee bar. I don't know why a cruise ship needs a coffee bar but apparently, they count as an amenity nowadays. Our Doris is fond of the place because it hasn't succumbed to popular demand and rather than be a poorly-lit hole dedicated to bad wall art and jazz music taken straight from television's favourite adverts, the ship's coffee bar was airy, and the only sound came from the buzz of patrons chatting over their cappuccinos – a throwback to the nineteen-eighties. I imagine thirty years ago you'd have found them doing business over coffee, sealing deals – fulfilling every yuppie ideal of the time. Our Doris isn't too pleased about the fact that the tables are screwed down, but she lets things slide because of their cloth napkins.

We sat at our usual table with our drinks. I knew things weren't right when she ordered a latte. Our Doris is a staunch supporter of the cappuccino – says as a latte has that much milk it's basically a beverage for those who've lost control of their waistline with little to no self-esteem.

Not that our Doris has much self-esteem left. After having most of her hair burned off trying to save Reuben from a firework, and losing a WI leadership contest to Pandra O'Malley, she's become a bit more quiet – distant some might say.

Before we came on the cruise, she started to let me read the Daily Mirror in public. We had Chinese takeaway three times in four weeks, and she said nothing when I offended her cousin Mavis. It never quite came to the point that she needed to listen to rock music, but it came close enough that I hid her Meat Loaf CDs. There's only so many times a man can hear *I Would Do Anything for Love* before he begins to question whether he actually would.

I let our Doris mull over her latte before saying to her, I said, 'Why is it such an issue if someone had the same idea as you?'

I half-expected the Look but our Doris said, 'It's not that someone had the same idea as me. It's because it serves to emphasise that I am behind the times.'

I have to admit, this left me completely befuddled. I said to her, I said, 'Well, now I can tell you're definitely off your rocker. What do you mean – behind the times? You've got yourself on Instagram – you've even been checking up on Netflix for crying out loud.'

'That is because it has completely revolutionised the way we watch television so don't you get like that with me, Harold Copeland. I like to keep abreast of popular culture but that doesn't mean I'm not a bit slow on the uptake.'

'You had a Sky box before anyone else on our street.'

'Why can't you just let me wallow, our 'arold? A

supportive husband would let his wife wallow.'

'Give over, our Doris – no man sits there whilst his wife is feeling sorry for herself and does nothing to help. You're Doris Copeland – you once set up an Easter egg hunt for the under-tens with no council backing, during a chicken pox outbreak.'

This brought a glimmer of a smile to her lips, it were barely a twitch but it was there. She sighed, set her shoulders back, looked me straight in the eye and said to me, she said, 'It's moments like this that remind me why I married you.'

I said, 'You're sure it wasn't my sheer sex appeal?'

This really got her laughing. She flung back her head and let a guffaw burst from deep within her chest. This wasn't the chuckle she saved for public engagement, this wasn't even the laugh she shared in private, this was a full-blown, all guns blazing, belly laugh – the kind you'd expect from a bloke down the pub after a dirty joke, not the kind you'd expect from a seventy-four year old housewife from Cheshire.

Once she settled down, I said to her, I said, 'I don't see what's so funny.'

She gave me a look, all flirty and mischievous, and said to me, she said, 'You're seventy-six and have a face like a turnip. If I didn't love you, I'd have traded you in for Richard Gere years ago.'

I smiled at this and said, 'That about borders on a compliment, does that, our Doris.'

'Don't get used to it,' she said.

After a few minutes I thought I'd broach the subject of her notice. 'Just what is a hat club anyway?'

'If you hadn't noticed, since that fool Emmeline burned off most of my hair, I have been experimenting with various forms of headwear in the hopes of detracting from the fact that my scalp currently looks like a field gone fallow.'

'It's not that bad.'

'It looks like I've dandelion seeds for hair, our 'arold. As my husband you have to view me with rose-tinted glasses – you don't notice any of my flaws or imperfections.'

I hadn't the heart to tell her that I had noticed but any husband worth his salt keeps these things from his wife. If she asks if there are more crow's feet around her eyes you point out the poor lighting in the bathroom and declare a mild case of conjunctivitis.

I said to our Doris, I said, 'So you decided to start a hat club because you're looking for new ways to dress your head?'

She sighed that sigh I've come to associate with our Doris's utter disappointment in my knowledge of societal expectations, and said to me, she said, 'When I wear a hat or scarf indoors, people stare. Now, I am no stranger to being the topic of conversation. When one has been at the centre of so many storms, one becomes used to it. I also have the necessary knowledge to take charge of these situations. Therefore, rather than allow anyone to even consider questioning my choice of headwear, I create a club that draws attention to my issue explicitly. I also make it a pre-requisite that anyone who joins the group has to decorate their scalp as a requirement.'

'But now there's already a group in place, what do you do?'

She became that intent on thought she didn't pay attention to the foam moustache she'd gained. She looked like Leonard Pierce as she said, 'First I have to find out just who this Mrs Veronica Ambrose is. She'll have reasons of her own for starting her club, and it is my duty as a concerned patron of this luxury liner to find out what they are.'

I handed her a napkin so as she could clean herself up and said, 'You get my heart going when you behave like a mob boss, our Doris. This Veronica Ambrose won't know what she's got herself into.'

Our Doris began her quest as soon as we arrived back in our cabin. She found her iPad and FaceTimed Theo. He wasn't best pleased at being woken up, but our Doris pointed out it was eleven o'clock in the UK and he really had no reason to complain. 'Besides,' she said, 'we've discussed this, our Theo, and I thought we'd agreed you wouldn't subscribe to millennial ideas of teenage idleness.'

'What do you want, Nan?' he asked, yowling worse than a cat in a dustbin.

'Don't you want to ask me how I am?' Our Doris offered her simpering tones, the kind grandmothers have perfected over the generations in the name of emotionally blackmailing their grandchildren to do their bidding.

Our Theo clearly hadn't noticed as he said to her, he said, 'No. You haven't fallen overboard. Grandad's wearing a tie. At your age if you're not in a box when you wake up then you're okay.'

Our Doris bristled. She pressed her tongue against

the back of her teeth and said, 'Whilst I clearly telephoned at the wrong time –'

'You didn't telephone.'

'I beg your pardon.'

'You FaceTimed, you didn't telephone.'

I took charge here. I saw our Doris's shoulders heave, all set to unleash utter fury on our Theo for his insolence. I said to him, I said, 'Right, Theo, we know you're a teenage lad, you don't need to keep acting like it. Your Nan needs your help, and as she's been telling everyone on this ship what a young gentleman you are, you might want to act on it.'

He looked a bit puzzled to be honest. I've no idea if it were tiredness or him being a bit gormless but our Doris had caught on to what I were doing because she said to him, she said, 'Well, you're joining us when we reach Lisbon and suppose I were to infer that your mother found an unsavoury magazine beneath your mattress? It could very well colour their view of you before you've met them.'

There was a moment when it looked like we had him – genuine worry widened his eyes and had him gulp before a new expression settled on his face, a calculating look our Doris couldn't help but be proud of. He said to us, he said, 'At first, I guess I'll tell them I got the magazine from Alf. My main grandfatherly figure has absconded on a three-month cruise with little thought as to the mental wellbeing of his only grandson, and as such I had no choice but to turn to your best friend for advice.

'I could even let it slip that this trip is a celebration for the end of Nan's community service. Also, considering we are now living in a sex positive society, it would be quite easy for me to challenge the outdated views of my own grandparents as they sought to involve me in their attempts to commit underhanded deeds.'

He grinned at us then. 'I might be tired, but I'm not stupid.'

In that moment I were terrified of my grandson. Not only had he successfully turned our blackmail attempt on us, but he had done it effortlessly, as though it were always there, bubbling beneath the surface.

Our Doris has taught him well.

If he doesn't make a politician, he'll make a great tax dodger.

Either way, his threat had clearly brightened his morning because he sat bolt upright, eyes alert and said, 'So, what can I do you for?'

'There's no need to use such common parlance, our Theo. The reason I contacted you is because I need information, and you're the only person I know who could do so and maintain the utmost discretion.' Our Doris clearly hoped complimenting him might prevent him revealing our secrets to all and sundry. That's the problem with grandchildren: they've memories like sponges. They never forget. You can accidentally step on their megazord in two-thousand-and-two and they'd quite happily use it against you in a court of law as evidence of your character.

Our Theo asked, 'What do you need me to find out?'

'There's a lady on the ship – Mrs Veronica Ambrose. I want you to find out all you can about her and ring me back.'

He grinned, revealing a perfect smile. At least his braces had done a good job, he looked ever the pearlescent shark as he said to our Doris, he said, 'Are you snooping again, Nan?'

Her eyes went wide at this. She practically inhaled her lips they pursed that tight. 'I have never been a snoop.'

'Is she snooping again, Grandad?' His grin wouldn't dissipate.

I wasn't rising to it. I said to him, I said. 'She happens to be your grandmother, our Theo. Don't be so cheeky.'

I could see he were hopeful that our Doris were back to her old tricks, but I wasn't prepared to make any announcements just yet. There was every chance our Doris could easily slip back into the doldrums and find herself blaring Jon Bon Jovi on the iPad at three o'clock in the morning.

We made our goodbyes and our Theo disappeared to go and find out all he could about Mrs Veronica Ambrose.

I knew that our Doris wouldn't be able to wait for Theo though. She set the iPad down on her desk and said to me, she said, 'All right then, our 'arold. I want you to go down to the bar and ask that new pal of yours for information.'

'Isn't this a bit much, our Doris? She's just one woman. You could always go down to this hat club and see what it's all about.'

'I'm afraid that isn't an option, our 'arold. One must know the terrain before one chooses to traverse upon it.'

'Terrain? It's the dining hall.'

'Perhaps I did not choose my words wisely, but if I'd wanted grammatical lessons, I'd have called Stephen Fry.' She straightened her lapels and said, 'I will go and speak to several reliable sources, and hopefully garner some knowledge as to just who this woman thinks she is.'

'I'm guessing we won't be playing whist this afternoon then?'

Our Doris gave me a smile so thin she looked like a serpent. 'If you'd hurry up and do as I ask, then you may just get the opportunity.'

I suppose I had no choice. I set out.

The bar onboard had been styled like the classic British pub; everything was teak. There were green cushioned benches and despite the fluorescent lights, I could pretend I was back in Partridge Mews. At least I could if it wasn't for the chirpy-faced bar staff, and the ship's constant movement.

I ordered a pint of bitter and chose my usual table.

It didn't take long for him to appear, materialising in thin air like some sort of TARDIS.

Percy.

If our Doris hadn't mentioned confidentiality earlier, I'd be certain Percy had one of the staff notify him of my arrival. It seems I only have to walk into the bar and he appears. My very own spectre of perpetual happiness: Percy.

He's an all right lad. Fifty-seven years old with all his own teeth, and a full head of hair. He's in better shape than I was at his age, which might have something to do with him going to the gym five times a week, and that he bypasses every offer of bacon in favour of natural yoghurt.

I've no idea why since the only benefit I've found from natural yoghurt is it takes the heat out of chicken tikka masala.

Percy sat across from me, his half pint of soda water fizzing away on the table beside my pint. There were something like shame rattling in my chest. He said to me, he said, 'How do, Harry? I didn't see you at Hot Yoga this morning.'

'Hot Yoga? What the bleeding heck is Hot Yoga?'

One day I swear something will wipe the smile off Percy's face. It's always there. A constant reminder that he only lives life on the edge when he puts honey in his green tea. For now he simply chuckled, and said, 'I didn't realise just how addled you were last night. We were discussing the benefits of Hot Yoga and you said as though you believed that wife of yours would find the idea of her husband participating in a multicultural exercise regime quite agreeable.'

I felt all the colour leave my face. I must have been more drunk than I thought if I were talking like our Doris. The worst part was I could remember every word. Percy brought it up, made his impassioned appeal, including the information that the classes were full of middle-aged women in various states of health and undress, and it may be in keeping with my interests. Apparently, I've talked one too many times about Charlie Dimmock.

Not that it mattered because I'd completely forgotten all about it. I said to him, I said, 'Sorry about that, Percy, the more I thought about coming, the more I realised it might not be the best thing for my new knee.'

'On the contrary, yoga is a great form of exercise for

anyone suffering with rheumatic pain.'

'That's just the thing. My knee's not used to such activity – it may become accustomed to better treatment, and we can't be having that.'

Even the way Percy slurped his soda water annoyed me. He drank it like a sommelier, as though there were assorted flavours of nothing. 'If you want to have a good few final years on this earth, then you could do worse than take some light exercise.'

I nodded. There isn't much else a man can do in such a situation than nod. It's the habit of most healthy people is advising others on how best to improve their quality of life. The best response is to smile and nod. There's no point telling them about my Uncle Frank, who never had a drop of cholesterol in his life and still got hit by a bus the week before his forty-fifth birthday.

All Percy's talk of Hot Yoga gave me a brainwave. I said to him, I said, 'You wouldn't happen to know if there's a Veronica Ambrose at this exercise class of yours, would you?'

He thought about this for a moment before saying, he said, 'Veronica? No, I don't know a Veronica, but then I've not really been going that long. I prefer Zumba.'

'I thought as much.'

'What makes her a person of interest?'

'She's starting some sort of club our Doris is interested in.'

'And Doris wants to know just what makes Veronica tick before she goes about committing to anything?'

'That's about the measure of it, yeah.' I said. I'd nearly finished my bitter and I were no closer to finding out about the mysterious Veronica Ambrose.

'I could ask around and see if anyone has heard

about her?'

'Thanks,' I said, 'I get the feeling she doesn't particularly want anyone knowing about her.'

'You get all sorts on these cruises – she could be an agoraphobic.'

'She's starting a club.'

'An enigma. Ever likely she likes to create a spectacle. From what you've told me she might not be too dissimilar to your Doris.'

I finished my drink. Percy had hit the nail on the head. I didn't mind trying to figure out who Mrs Ambrose was, it was the thought there was another Doris in the world that really got me sweating.

After listening to Percy harp on about the healing properties of kale, I returned to the cabin.

Our Doris sat in the armchair watching Murder, She Wrote, but she wasn't paying attention. Her eyes were glazed over. Either she were mulling things over or she'd had a sudden attack of glaucoma.

It took a few seconds for her to even notice I'd arrived. She said to me, she said, 'You didn't find anything out then?' Despite her glum tone, there was something hopeful in her voice.

I shook my head. 'Percy's never heard of her. He's going to ask around.'

Her eyes flew back into her head at this point. She clenched the arms of her chair as every one of her wrinkles tightened. 'What the bleeding heck have you let him do that for, our 'arold? I need to remain discreet. I can't have it getting around that I'm asking questions about Mrs Ambrose. Suppose news gets back to her? We must always be ahead of the game. Otherwise, we run the risk of appearing uncouth and quite ignorant of societal niceties. Just look at the welcome party fiasco. I'll never look at Mrs Hebblethwaite the same.'

'I don't think anyone will.'

The welcome party was hosted by the ship's staff in the main conference room. They'd decorated with banners, and there were a revolving stream of adverts about the cruise company's boats and tours on several televisions around the room. Not that they could be heard. Whoever was in charge of music kept playing songs from the nineteen-eighties. I mean, I've no problem with Kylie Minogue but when you're crammed into a stifling hot room full of OAPs and middle-aged retirees, all chatting their nonsense you don't feel very lucky at all.

We'd been there for three quarters of an hour when Mrs Hebblethwaite walked in. If a jumbo jet and a double-decker bus ever had a baby it would be Mrs Hebblethwaite. She is humungous. She pushed past people to get to the buffet table, wearing a floral kaftan that large she could have clothed half of Rotherham. Now, I'm not fat-shaming – she's probably a beautiful person on the inside, buried deep beneath her subcutaneous fat. Or she has a thyroid condition. I don't know. All I do know is that she commandeered a quiche meant to feed twelve people, ate it, and then openly claimed it lacked flavour and she was concerned about the risk of salmonella.

Once she ate her fill, she decided she wanted to dance. There was no room to dance. People barely had space to chat. If it weren't for necessity it would have looked like there were a dozen extra-marital affairs going on in that conference room.

Without caring who she bumped into, Mrs

Hebblethwaite began to dance. It looked something like the twist – there were a few kicks and every now and then a finger wag. I figure she can't be any further than her early sixties.

I suppose we should have known how it would go.

The sweat built on her brow and flowed down her nose like Niagara Falls in a monsoon. Her skin paled as she danced, and I suppose something of the green hue blossomed on her cheeks.

Folk soon grew fed up of her constantly knocking into them and asked one of the staff to say something.

A young girl squeezed her way over and tapped Mrs Hebblethwaite on the shoulder. She said to her, she said, 'Excuse me, madame, but I will have to ask you to stop doing whatever it is you're doing, as you're upsetting other residents and it is our aim to make sure all feel as though this is their home.'

Mrs Hebblethwaite clasped the girl's shoulders and was all set to say something when she threw up.

She completely covered the girl from head to toe in thick, yellow vomit. The stench added to the already musky, sweaty odour that filled the conference room.

Most left after the vomiting. Apparently, it's a health and safety nightmare nowadays, and nobody wanted to risk infection, despite the fact they'd seen her attack the mountain of quiche beforehand.

Our Doris was appalled and said as if Mrs Hebblethwaite had considered the socioeconomic standing of her fellow ship mates, she'd have recognised that her sort were more suited to Butlins than a five star cruise liner with a choice of four swimming pools and spa facilities.

She even went so far as to write a letter to the CEO of the cruise company advising them to properly vet all their residents before booking to avoid such embarrassing episodes happening again. She didn't get a reply, but we did get champagne with breakfast the next morning; I never imagined black pudding would pair well with Moet de Chandon.

At first, I'd been surprised by our Doris's actions. Since she became friends with Erin, I thought she'd turned over a new leaf, had gained some more appreciation for those she deems lower class than herself. I can't help but wonder whether it was just Mrs Hebblethwaite's class that had our Doris furious, or whether she had some other reason for bemoaning the woman's presence on the ship.

All this about Mrs Hebblethwaite led my thoughts down a different avenue. We were all packed that tight in the conference room there's no telling who we were bumping into.

I said to our Doris, I said, 'Could Mrs Ambrose have been at the welcome party?'

'No.'

'You told me it was compulsory.'

'For you it was.'

'Are you telling me I could have stayed in the bar watching the cricket?'

Our Doris gave me the Look and said, 'I did not raise an unsociable husband, our 'arold. If you'd taken the time to read the welcome pack, like I asked, you'd have known that whilst the party was open to all guests to get to know one another, they weren't required to attend.'

'You lied to me, our Doris.'

'I did, and no doubt I'll do it again, so it's best not to waste time pretending you expected more from me.'

That much was true. Our Doris has always got her

own way. I shouldn't think because we're on our jollies she would be any different.

She went on to tell me that she had learned from outside sources that Mrs Veronica Ambrose was staying in the Liberty Suite, the most prestigious of all suites – by this our Doris meant the most expensive, but she's always thought money equals quality, despite the fact I've used off-brand denture adhesive for years without complaint – Mrs Ambrose had so far eluded most of the women on board, as well as Cyril Marsden, which was probably for the best, really.

'So no one knows who she is?'

Our Doris paced back and forth across the carpet, like I don't know what. It were like being back home. If she carried on, she'd do more than tear a hole in the carpet, she'd burrow straight through to the cabin below, and probably wouldn't stop until she reached the boiler room – she'd think nothing of us getting charged for reupholstery.

She had this look about her, eyes pierced and calculating, like a vulture, before saying, she said, 'It's smart. This is a woman who clearly knows what she's doing when it comes to increasing interest in a new club. All people know about her is that she has money and an interest in millinery.

'I had purely selfish reasons for beginning my club, but just what motivated Mrs Ambrose is what I want to know.'

'What's the plan then, our Doris? Do we go to her suite?'

'Whilst this would be suitable if she were residing in a common cabin, our 'arold, we can hardly go calling on a suite unannounced, it is against all rules of social decorum.'

'Well, what are you going to do then?'

Our Doris dropped down into a chair and exhaled a breath so forceful she could've blown over Blackpool Tower. Her eyes were as beady as a squirrel's as she said to me, she said, 'It's no use sending her an invitation to a spot of tea in our cabin. Shelagh O'Reilly tried that and didn't even get a no thank you.'

'We could fake a survey. That worked when you wanted to see Mrs Pritchard-Singh's new wallpaper.'

'Yes, but I know her. It's different. If she didn't let me in, then Margaret Witstanley wouldn't have invited her to her supper party. Besides, Mrs Pritchard-Singh wanted to show that wallpaper to anyone passing. You may recall reports of her calling the milkman indoors at five o'clock in the morning to show him the wonders of B&Q's premium designs.'

I avoided any mention of the milkman. A thought had sprung unbidden into my mind and I felt no choice but to voice it, I said to our Doris, I said, 'Wait a minute, our Doris, where does Mrs Ambrose go at meal times?'

Our Doris nodded and said, 'I spoke to one of the kitchen staff who informed me that she cannot break client confidentiality by supplying that information but I may be pleased to hear that all residents are well-looked after and receive the full care and attention from a team of highly-trained staff members who service their every want and need.'

'Which leaves you no closer to an answer.'

'Thank you, our 'arold, I always know I can count on you to point out the blindingly obvious.'

Later that day our Theo got in touch to tell us the only trace of Mrs Veronica Ambrose was an article about how she raised a few thousand pounds for her local youth hostel. Even that didn't give a clear indication as to who she was as there was no picture because a swan had done a few tricks on a trampoline and became the story of the week.

Our Doris didn't sleep that night.

I know because the room wasn't filled with the sound of a pneumatic drill on concrete.

I've grown accustomed to our Doris's snoring over time. It's almost a lullaby is our Doris's snoring. And considering she's always said she's determined I'll go before her I knew it was insomnia plaguing our Doris rather than anything deadly.

I had no choice. I put my teeth back in and switched on my bedside lamp.

What I saw disturbed me to my very core and I saw Psycho the first time around.

Our Doris sat up in bed, the light from her lamp casting a green glow on her vampiric pale skin. Only it wasn't her skin. Whatever it was made her cheeks look as though they were melting. She had her hands clasped on top of the duvet and stared straight at the wall.

I said to her, concerned, I said, 'Are you all right, our Doris?'

'I'm perfectly fine, our 'arold. I was struggling to

sleep. The iPad recommended I try a face mask and I happened to recall that one was included in our complimentary bag of toiletries, and now I'm watching the clock because I'm certain this will not cure my sleeplessness, but it will definitely cause some skin irritation.'

'Why didn't you wash it off immediately?'

'Because I wanted to see whether it would help me sleep. If it doesn't I will write a strongly worded letter to the website owners to inform them their advice is no good and I demand a retraction.'

'You've been planning the letter since you put the mask on, haven't you?'

She grumbled. Her chin dropped, smearing the strange concoction as she said to me, she said, 'It's no business of yours what I've been planning, our 'arold, but in this instance you are correct.'

'Well there's one problem. You're supposed to spend the time relaxing, forgetting trivial matters, not planning war against folk who only offered advice in the first place.'

'It is my duty as a concerned citizen to test these things.'

'You're only doing it so you can promote Oil of Olay.'

'It's never kept me awake at night though, has it?'

'You and I both know the only thing keeping you awake is Veronica Ambrose.'

'You're getting very presumptuous now we're at sea. I should hope you won't be bringing this new attitude home with you.'

'Night, our Doris.' I removed my dentures and switched off the lamp.

I slept more soundly knowing our Doris was awake

beside me. Pirates wouldn't even consider attacking a ship with her on board.

I thought she would have been dead on her feet the next day, but found myself awoken at half past seven, our Doris looming over me, my trousers in her hands. If there were bags under her eyes, I couldn't see them, maybe the face mask had worked more than she anticipated. She still had her wrinkles, but she had something of the glow about her. She said to me, she said, 'I've let you sleep in long enough, our 'arold, I won't have it getting around that I don't know how to keep my husband to a rigorous schedule.'

I sat up, taking my trousers from her, and said to her, I said, 'I don't suppose you'll allow me the chance to shower first, our Doris?'

'On the contrary, I hoped you would shower. If you would be so kind as to use the new aftershave I purchased for you I would be quite pleased.'

Even if I'd had my teeth in, I think my grimace would have been as prominent. My lips sank into my face and I screwed up my face worse than a toddler being told he can't have an ice cream. I said, 'You know

I don't like that aftershave, our Doris.'

'Whether you like it or not means nothing to me. It has a distinguished perfume that adds an air of prestige to any middle-class gentleman.'

'What if I don't want to smell like a middle-class gentleman?'

'Considering you currently smell as though you've hiked from Macclesfield to Malaysia, I think you'd do well to use the aftershave.' With that she wandered over to the wardrobe and began to put together my outfit for the day.

Meanwhile I disappeared to the en-suite.

Once the regular morning ablutions were complete, I put on the aftershave our Doris insisted I use. I cannot stand it. It smells like a mixture of raspberries and musk and fox muck, or something else a dog will roll around in. But our Doris said as she wanted me to wear it, and I suppose that not doing so would result in a fate worse than death.

I didn't know if I were being punished for not sitting up awake with her, or if she had something planned, but I did know that I was going to spend the day stinking worse than a muck midden on the hottest day in summer.

On our stroll to the dining room, our Doris was as hawkish as Jessica Fletcher. She kept stopping every few moments to listen hard. She peered around corners, muttering to herself as she eyed the other passengers as though searching them for distinguishing features she could associate with the image she'd formed of Mrs Veronica Ambrose.

It took us about fifteen minutes to get to breakfast with all our Doris's meandering. We hadn't been sat at the table long when one of the younger staff members approached us — I recognised her instantly as the poor girl who'd been the victim of Mrs Hebblethwaite. She didn't seem to be suffering any long-lasting effects, and I hoped for her sake she'd been offered a pay rise.

She had a small smile on her face as she came over, that saleswoman smile — she was happy to help but would throw us overboard if we stepped out of line — and said to our Doris, she said, 'Good morning, Mrs Copeland, I hope you're well this morning. I have been asked to deliver this to you by another passenger.' She handed an envelope to our Doris and scuttled away as fast as she could, looking somewhat like a beetle making a hasty retreat.

Our Doris stared down at the small lavender envelope, at her name written in somewhat impressive calligraphy. She opened it and removed a piece of thick, cream notepaper. I was certain our Doris had got a letter from the Queen herself. Her eyes were wide as she started reading, slowly piercing until she were squinting at the note, her arms tense, muscles taut — looked set to tear apart the paper with all the strength of Tyson Fury.

I said to her, I said, 'What's the problem, our Doris?'

I'd been all set to properly inhale my Full English, but now our Doris looked ready to demolish downtown Tokyo with nothing more than a piece of notepaper and determination.

'I have been invited to attend the Hat Club by Mrs Veronica Ambrose.'

Our Doris gulped. She clenched the edge of the table, her fingers looking as though she'd contracted Reynaud's.

I said to her, I said, 'I thought you were planning to go anyway.'

She gave me the Look and said to me, she said, 'Of course I was planning to attend, our 'arold, but I intended to employ an air of uncertainty so that the women understood whilst I wish to be present, my time is in great demand and as such I cannot commit to anything too trivial. Now, however, I have been invited by the founder herself. Should I choose not to attend it will be seen as an insult to Mrs Ambrose, something I cannot very well risk when I do not know the circumstances of the individual.'

I sat, somewhat flabbergasted, before saying, 'What will you do now?'

'I've no choice. I'm going to have breakfast.'

I looked at her gone out. 'All right then.'

Our Doris returned the note to the envelope and slipped it inside her handbag. She looked at her meal dejectedly – this morning her poached eggs, smoked salmon and lightly toasted English breakfast muffin came with a side of disappointment. 'This wouldn't sustain Winston Churchill, let alone a white middle-class woman with a fast metabolism and a responsible diet.'

Within moments she was on her feet.

When she came back, she had a Full English breakfast on her plate, something she warned against because she said some of the more European passengers might think it an egregious display of gluttony. After the note, she clearly didn't care, she attacked her food like a Komodo dragon tearing apart a buffalo. She didn't let her first plate of food go to waste either, she practically swallowed it whole. I'd never seen our Doris so rattled, and that includes the time she found out Waitrose would be discontinuing her favourite brand of lapsang souchong.

I said to her, I said, 'Are you sure you should be eating so fast, our Doris?'

'I do not know if I am embarking upon a war, our 'arold. No one would enter into such a situation without a full stomach.' With that she allowed herself a small belch and proceeded to neck her cappuccino as though it were a pint of Boddington's Best. She handed me her cup and said to me, she said, 'Get me an espresso. I've got some preparation to do, and I need a clear head after the night I've had.'

Her preparations didn't amount to much really. She asked around a bit more to see if anyone had any new information, but no one had seen anything of Veronica Ambrose since we boarded.

A few days later our Doris attended the Hat Club.

The group met in the dining hall at breakfast. Our Doris had dressed for the occasion, in a floral print dress from John Lewis. It were white and covered with violets. She wrapped a lavender scarf around her head, before putting her white straw hat on top of that. All of this was given as much thought as a person takes when buying a car. Apparently, she worried about wearing purple as some of the other women in attendance may see this as an attempt from our Doris to flaunt that she believes herself above them by fashioning herself in what has been recognised as a regal colour since the dawn of time.

She also wore sunglasses.

I'm not sure why she wore sunglasses, perhaps it were an attempt at going incognito. Either way she wore sunglasses that covered the majority of her face, shielding her eyes from fluorescent lights whilst hiding the wrinkles on her forehead.

I ended up at a table with a whole host of other

husbands who'd been brought along to view the spectacle of their wives assembled at a large circular table near the omelette station, wearing an assortment of hats, fascinators and headscarves.

The women spoke to one another as animated as chickens in a coop, ruffling feathers and chatting nonsense.

After a few minutes, the doors of the hall opened, and the room went silent. One of the cruise workers announced, 'Good morning, ladies and gentlemen, it is my pleasure to introduce you all to a person you've all been yearning to know. Please can I ask you to give a very warm welcome to Mrs Veronica Ambrose.'

All eyes alighted upon the individual who chose to enter the room like an empress. She surveyed us all like we were ants in a jam jar – prepared to put the lid on and have us suffocate. It had been a long time since I'd seen anyone with as many chins as this woman, and that includes the time I accidentally walked into a Slimming World meeting on the way to church. I wasn't sure if she wore a dress or a pair of curtains.

The woman kept her face hidden beneath the brim of her purple straw hat. All I could make out was the colour of her lips. Purple. Deep purple. They contrasted against the white of her skin, so pale her skin could have been made from milk.

When she reached the table, she tipped her head back and gave the women a Look to rival that of our Doris.

And our Doris returned the Look with all the fury she could muster. Her eyes became mere dots in her face as she realised she did know Veronica. We all did.

Our Doris had despised the woman since she first discovered her presence, because Mrs Ambrose was none other than the great quiche devourer herself.

'I thought your name was Mrs Hebblethwaite,' our Doris said, her words tinged with enough growl to scare a chihuahua.

'Once upon a time it was, Mrs Copeland. That is your chosen moniker, I believe. I ought to recognise a woman who espouses such knowledge of social niceties in the letters she spends her days sending my way.' She allowed a small smile to resonate on her pursed lips.

The Look on our Doris's face slipped slightly. 'I'm afraid I have not an iota of an idea to the letters I supposedly sent to you.'

The other women at the table shared curious glances with one other, looking like a chorus line in some sort of am-dram production.

Mrs Ambrose, or Hebblethwaite, or whatever she wanted to be called, said to our Doris, she said, 'I suppose it was somewhat remiss of me not to offer you my name, age, and occupation when first we met, however one must get the measure of a person before they choose to make an acquaintance of them.

'See, I am Mrs Veronica Ambrose, nee Hebblethwaite, the owner of a prestigious cruise company whose ship you're currently using to explore the four corners of the world from the comfort of one of our rather luxurious cabins.

'I do not blame you for not knowing to whom you speak. I cannot expect someone of your calibre to properly vet the CEO of a cruise company before booking to avoid such embarrassment.' Mrs Ambrose sat down now, a twinkle in her eyes as she reached for a champagne flute on the table.

As soon as her fingers touched the glass, the waiters swept in to fill the glasses of all the ladies around the table.

Our Doris said to Mrs Ambrose, she said, 'On the contrary, Mrs Ambrose, once I discovered your presence upon the ship, I immediately asked my grandson to research your name. I'm afraid he could find out nothing about anyone sharing your details. Perhaps you used another of your aliases when documenting your successes or your company isn't as prestigious as you have led yourself to believe.'

'I am quite aware of my successes, Mrs Copeland, do not fret on that account. No, I understand your concerns relating to my activities at the welcome party. I behaved in a manner unbecoming of someone in my standing, which was one reason behind my offering you all champagne with breakfast.' At this point Mrs Ambrose faced the rest of the women. She allowed herself a sip of her drink before saying to them all, she said, 'It is true I created a spectacle at the welcome party. This is due, in part, to some ill news I received from my physician back home. One reason I chose to found this Hat Club is because I will soon lose my hair due to some treatment I will receive for a truly awful disease. I believe that many of you will have been touched by such horror previously and, as such, I chose to seek out likeminded individuals for support, and to show that I completely and irrevocably regret my actions.

'I have always had a penchant for baked goods and that quiche was no exception. Why I chose to dance after the fact is nobody's business but do know the decision was fuelled by a mixture of Babycham and despair.

'I hope you can all join me in raising a toast to celebrate the inaugural meeting of The Hat Club, a place in which we can support one another, and hopefully grow friendships whilst we traverse the glorious oceans our planet has to offer.'

Our Doris's lips were trembling. There were this mixture of fury and admiration on her face I hadn't seen since the speeches at our wedding when her father chose to give a speech only to end up thumping the vicar after he made one too many references to sheep.

The Hat Club raised their glasses to Mrs Ambrose whilst she and our Doris stared at each other. There was a veritable energy about them that could make them enemies, or the best of friends and I had no idea which way the tide would turn.

Percy chose that moment to appear at the table, sweating, and as breathless as a cross country runner in a heatwave. After downing a pint of water, he said to me, he said, 'I left Hot Yoga early. What did I miss?'

TWO

Our Doris says as we must appreciate people of all sizes nowadays, says as you can't warn a Weight Watcher with an onion ring halfway to their mouth that they're in danger of dying because it'll be seen as fat shaming. It's a delicate situation, apparently.

I only found all this out because I upset Ken from cabin eight. He's a big lad himself is Ken, not so fat as he can't get through the turnstile at Old Trafford but close enough.

Well, a few of us were at the bar of an evening, a bit three sheets to the wind, but nowhere near the blind drunkenness they warn against on a cruise ship, when Ken said as he could do with another pint.

At which point I said to him, purely in jest, believing a grown man of sixty-eight could take a joke, I said, 'You've already got the beer belly, are you going for the full barrel?'

And he laughed. He laughed right at my face, before going to his Sheila and saying I was judgmental, fat shaming, and had ultimately emotionally scarred him.

He even went so far as to see the ship's therapist.

I'd have thought Ken would have more sense about him, knowing my wife. Maybe he really wanted to see me punished, see me face the full force of our Doris's wrath.

If he did, he'd have been disappointed.

When our Doris told me how Ken felt she didn't give me the Look, not straight away anyway. She didn't pace the carpet looking like a malfunctioning Theresa May.

No, our Doris did something much worse than that.

She treated me like I'd gone senile.

There comes a time in every couple's marriage when one ends up parenting the other. Our Doris started on our wedding day. The ring had barely touched her finger before she straightened my bow tie and said to me, she said, 'I cannot bear the idea of an unkempt husband, our 'arold. You really should strive to look your best at all times.'

Being quite honest, our Doris said a lot to me on our wedding day, and I did everything she said thinking about our wedding night. I was also a bit blinded by adoration and too much Dutch courage at the Hare and Horse before the ceremony.

Either way, we were sat in our cabin, on the edge of the bed, and our Doris actually took my hands in hers, as though she were all set to tell me she were leaving me for Herbert Kettlewell and his menagerie of parrots and Tiswas memorabilia.

She spoke in this sombre tone, the kind doctors adopt to deliver bad news, as she said to me, she said, 'Sheila has informed me of your little social faux pas, our 'arold.'

I said, 'What're you talking about?'

'I must say I understand your puzzlement entirely.'

'Is this about Ken?'

'Am I right in believing you made a rather barbed comment in reference to his ever-expanding waistline?'

I must admit I stared at her all agog. I'd planned to spend the afternoon watching Guardians of the Galaxy whilst our Doris went to the spa and now I were stuck in bed with our Doris educating me on the correct way to address an overweight OAP.

I said to her, I said, 'I might've joked about the gut on him but that's all it were. Men take the mick out of each other, our Doris, it's part of being a man. One day I get one in about his weight, the next he's mocking my ability to play cards.'

'Yes, well. Your pitiful poker face side, I'm afraid it just isn't the thing anymore.'

'What isn't?'

'Joking. Specifically jokes about a person's weight. In a multicultural, multigendered society, we must be accepting of people of all shapes and sizes, and whilst jokes regarding weight have always been commonplace, they have been made without consideration of the inner turmoil, or lack thereof, of people struggling, or not, with their weight. Therefore, you'd have been better off saying nothing about Ken's weight. For whilst he laughed at the time, he was actually hiding years' worth of pain.'

She patted my hand then.

I said to her, I said, 'Is he honestly upset?'

'Sheila says he's quite inconsolable, questioning just what you think of him.'

'I think he's a grade A pillock is what I think,' I said.

'Oh, I quite agree. One shouldn't have to censor oneself if no offence is meant, but we live in a world where the audience must all be appeased. With this in mind, I think it best if you apologise.'

I said to her, I said, 'I can tell you that won't be happening.'

Our Doris squeezed my hands a bit too tight and said to me, she said, 'I know it will happen, because if it doesn't happen, I will personally see that you spend the rest of this cruise going on early morning jogs with Percy.'

She might have given me the Look. I'm not too sure. I were focused on my hands trapped in the iron grip of our Doris.

I said to her, I said, 'Can't I just push him overboard?'

She looked me up and down and said, 'Great minds think alike – only I wasn't thinking about Ken.'

I ended up going to meet Percy in the spa. I wanted a pint but he fancied a matcha infused green smoothie with a ton of kale, full of antioxidants, roughage, and arrogance, drunk with a smile of satisfaction, not because he enjoyed the taste of blended canal water, but because he could show off that he's a level four health care nut.

I must have looked at him a bit funny because he said as if I wanted to prolong my life I needed to take better care of my body.

I said to him, I said, 'I have all my own teeth.'

'You have dentures,' he said.

'I paid for them, didn't I?' I knew I sounded a bit like Alf, but I couldn't help it. There's something about being cast adrift in the middle of the ocean that really causes you to appreciate what you have back home.

Our respective grandsons had offered to set up a Skype call for us but we declined.

You never know who else is watching.

I might think I'm having a private chat with an old

friend only to discover I've accidentally broadcast my secret for good geraniums to half of Indonesia.

Besides, the cruise only lasts three months.

That's barely any time at all is that.

I left home with the knowledge that if Brian Aldridge came up with a great get rich scheme in March, he'd still be trying to convince Jennifer in June. But that's The Archers for you. It's reliable. Not like these television soaps. I swear when I went in for my knee operation, they changed half the cast of Emmerdale.

I said to Percy, I said, 'If you fell overboard tomorrow, would you regret all this keep fit nonsense?'

He thought about this for a moment, gazing up at the strip lights as though some gremlin would emerge and give him the answer.

He looked me dead in the eye and said, 'No. And do you want to know why, Harry?'

I said I weren't fussed either way.

He said, 'People would say my death was a tragedy. That for someone who loved life so much it was a shame for theirs to be cut short.'

'What a load of old flannel.'

'Maybe, but at least I could have an open casket.'

'What are you trying to say?'

'That the best you can hope for is an old picture of you in your obituary. Maybe something prehistoric.' And there was that smug smile of satisfaction. He hadn't even needed to sip his murky smoothie.

I decided talk of death probably weren't the best place for my thoughts, so I said to him, I said, 'Have you heard about Ken?'

'Fat Ken Ken?'

I nodded. 'That's the one.'

'What about him?'

'He doesn't like being called fat.'

'But he is fat.'

'He doesn't like folk bringing it up.' That's when I told him my side of the story.

I suppose one good thing about Percy is that he'll actually sit and listen to you before deciding to chime in with his own story.

Percy nodded his head, all thoughtful like. Solemn, some might say. He chewed the hangnail of his left thumb with all the intensity of Paul Hollywood over a macaroon, before saying to me, he said, 'It's a classic case of denial, Harry.'

'It is?'

'It is. Ken knows he's fat. He's got to. You don't get up in the morning with a gut like his and think you're the pinnacle of health and vitality.'

'Unlike you.'

'Well yes, but my body has taken years of work. I haven't touched a Mars bar since nineteen-eighty-seven.'

'I suppose you went for tofu instead.'

'I did develop a peculiar fondness for cacao-infused tofu, but I slowed down. Too much protein.

'Anyway, with regards to Ken, he's the type of person that if he ate broccoli on Tuesday, he'd have a cream cake on Wednesday to congratulate himself.'

'So, because he's losing weight, I've got to deny he's fat, or has ever been fatter?'

'Even the term fat is out the window.'

'What else am I supposed to call him?'

'Stocky.'

'Stocky?'

'Stocky.'

'But he isn't stocky. Stocky is for somebody broad, muscular, like Marlon Brando or Fatima Whitbread. Ken isn't stocky, he's fat. He's fat enough to be Jabba the Hut's body double.'

'You might want to employ a bit of tact though, Harry. It doesn't hurt you to call him stocky.'

'Whose side are you on?'

'There is no side here. No matter your intent you offended him. And though we know he's eating himself into an early grave we have to respect his prerogative to remain blissfully oblivious.'

I said to him, I said, 'It's always been our Doris's job to be socially aware.'

'Didn't she get done for assault?'

'I never said she was good at it.'

I realised I had no other option.

I had to apologise. Though it made my blood boil more than a kettle in hot pants, I left Percy and made my way to Ken's cabin.

It was much the same as mine and our Doris's cabin, except theirs came with an odour of vegetable fat and stale flatulence. The sort of stink I expect from Theo, not a middle-aged couple with ties to Sainsbury's and a portable DVD player.

Sheila answered the door. When she saw it were me, her face did this thing where her eyes shrank, until they were little more than pieces of coal in her eye sockets.

I could have been staring into the void, some vacuum that would zap my insides and turn my brain to mush … or something like that. I don't know much about interstellar phenomena. If I were to end up in a Star Trek type situation, I'd be one of those fools in a redshirt.

Sheila looked at me like a fishmonger about to decapitate a haddock, and she said to me, she said,

'What the heck do you want?'

I have to admit, I were flummoxed. The air had left my lungs, and whilst I must be over a foot taller than Sheila, I felt like a schoolboy facing the headmistress. I wouldn't look amiss if I started wringing a flat cap in my hands. Not that I have a flat cap. Our Doris won't let me have a flat cap because she says they make an old man look past his sell-by. But if I did have a flat cap, I'd sure as damn it be wringing the beggar.

'Well?' Sheila said.

I couldn't bear it any longer. I steeled my courage, and said to her, I said, 'I've come to speak to your Ken.'

'You can't.'

'Oh.' I gave it a moment before saying, 'Why?'

She offered a fake laugh and rolled her eyes. All theatrical. She'd do all right on Coronation Street would Sheila. I can just imagine her tossing a pint over some unfortunate so-and-so.

'You must be joking,' she said, 'Ken doesn't want to see you. This business has really affected his emotional wellbeing. He's gained three pounds from the stress of it all.'

'He gained three pounds from pies is what he gained three pounds from.' Our Doris stepped into view, looking as irked as a snake denied a wildebeest. She'd gone for the pale pink headscarf, the one she said gave her a friendly, almost approachable air whilst looking chic and somewhat reminiscent of the Hollywood starlets of our youth. Clearly, she wasn't feeling too friendly at that moment. She fixed Sheila with a glare to rival Jeremy Corbyn.

'What're you doing here?' I asked our Doris.

She flashed the Look in my direction and said to me, she said, 'I came to talk to Sheila here regarding the business between you and her husband. You and I both know you were making jest about Ken's weight as you're worried about his health and wish for him to remain on this planet much longer. However, it now transpires that Sheila cares as much about her husband's ever-expanding waistline as Ann Widdecombe does feather dusters.'

'And what's that supposed to mean?' Sheila said.

'I'm most apologetic, I completely forgot that you care little for anything other than allowing your husband to guzzle enough bacon there's practically an entire pig reforming in his stomach.' Our Doris allowed herself a moment to breathe before continuing, she said, 'What I'm saying Sheila is that you don't care. You do not care about your husband. Perhaps you hope he'll eat himself into an early grave. Perhaps you have taken out a life insurance policy on the poor fellow, and hope that if you fill him with enough fat, he'll be killed off and you can use the money to get a manicure that doesn't leave you looking like you're descended from a bird of prey.'

I'd find out just what had got our Doris riled, later. At that moment, I had to concern myself with getting her out of there.

At least, I would have done, had a mere squeak of a voice not spoken from inside the cabin. 'I am here, you know?' Ken said.

I stepped over the threshold, pushing past Sheila to get a better look at the man I'd apparently caused untold emotional damage to. He lounged in a floral armchair, his too-tight polo shirt flashing the lower half of his hairy gut.

'You're eating a trifle!' I couldn't keep the incredulity from my voice. I heard the raise in pitch as though it belonged to another person, as though I had been possessed by the spirit of John Inman.

Ken had a large bowl on his lap, filled with enough trifle to feed an entire Christening party, and he was eating it with a tablespoon, lifting mountains of cream, and custard, and jelly into his fat gob. He stared at me, looking like a lad whose been caught fiddling with something he shouldn't. And he said to me, he said, 'It's your fault.'

'Exactly,' Sheila affirmed with a nod of her head. She had her hands on her hips. 'If you don't mind, I've had to order some room service because my husband is in such a state of distress, he can't possibly face leaving the cabin.'

'Why would he? That trifle's enough to keep a family of five going for a week.' I could not believe my eyes. The words were on my tongue before I could stop them, I said to him, I said, 'Why are you doing this to yourself, Ken?'

'I told you –'

'No. You used me as an excuse for your overeating. I've only known you for a couple of months, Ken. I'm pretty sure you were this big when you first set foot on deck.'

He gulped, looking to Sheila for support.

'How long have you been fat?' said our Doris.

'He's not fat!' Sheila protested.

'Have you had your cataracts checked recently?'

'I haven't got cataracts.'

'It must be love.' Our Doris sniffed and glanced at the floor. When she next spoke, we all had to strain to hear her, she said, 'Only if my husband was an advertisement for unbridled gluttony, I couldn't just stand idly by waiting for the inevitable heart attack, the admonition from my peers for not putting him on a diet sooner.'

'There's the difference between you and I,' Sheila said, believing she had the upper hand, 'I don't care what people think.'

And this is where our Doris smiled. This smile were more fearsome than when she saw the price of coffee in St. Mark's Square. It fills her eyes with this kind of wild gleefulness, not dissimilar to the way a cat looks after terrorising a nest of sparrows. She said to Sheila, she said, 'You might not, but he does, he told us himself not five minutes ago.

'Are you sure you don't simply prefer a fat man? I've heard less vicarious wives use this as a means to stop their husband getting up to mischief.'

Ken chose to speak up again. It was something of the shock really considering I'd completely forgotten he was there. 'I'm not fat,' he said.

Our Doris looked at him, startled. There was this curl of disbelief to her lips, giving her the look of Cesar Romero. 'I must apologise, Ken, I didn't realise they'd put funhouse mirrors in this cabin. If I were you, I'd ask for a refund.'

I said to her, I said, 'He doesn't like being called fat.'

'But he is fat.'

'He prefers the term stocky.'

The disbelief strained her entire face, causing the crow's feet around her eyes to expand to deep crevices. 'Stocky?' she said, 'The stockiest thing about him is the fetid stench of vegetable broth that follows him around.'

'I hope you're not talking about me,' Sheila interjected.

'Of course not, dear. You're barely worth talking

about.'

'You do know I'm in the room, right?'

'Once again, Ken. I could smell you from eight miles away, even with a bad case of sinusitis.'

'Where do you get off talking to my husband like that?'

I had to admire Sheila's sheer tenacity. Even when faced with the bear that is our Doris she barely even blinked.

Our Doris fixed Sheila with a look, a look that involved lips pursed tight enough to show only the most formidable wrinkles around her lips, and said to Sheila, she said, 'I do not find any pleasure in talking to your husband at all. I'm already contemplating a trip to the ship's therapist to discuss the trauma.'

'That's ridiculous,' Ken exclaimed, almost forgetting his trifle. 'I've never said anything insulting to you.'

'On the contrary, Kenneth, you mocked my headscarf.'

'You what?' I erupted immediately. I were Mount Vesuvius including the crags. I glowered at Ken, I'm fair certain I glowered as I said to him, I said, 'What in the Lord's name did you say about our Doris's headscarf?'

Ken became a turtle at that point. His neck sank down in his polo shirt until his ears balanced on the collar. He said to me, he said, 'I only said as it was a bit hot to be wearing it indoors.'

Sheila winced, hissing through her teeth. Even she knew her husband was guilty of something. I were about to ask him what he really said when our Doris piped up with, she said, 'I'm afraid that's not entirely correct. Is it, Sheila?'

The two of them were startled, there was no denying

that. It was a bit surreal to see our Doris doing her thing on a cruise ship. I didn't think she'd developed enough connection with anyone to be properly insulting.

I said to our Doris, I said, 'What did he say to you, our Doris?'

'I came here to try and prompt a reconciliation between you and Ken. You must admit you haven't made many acquaintances, and I worried this dispute could lead to your alienation from the small circle you've built.'

'All right,' I said, 'and what happened then?'

'I imagine that whilst Sheila lies to her husband on an hourly basis, she can't expect the same from me.'

'Hang on a minute. I'm no liar.'

'Let's not get into that again, Sheila. I'd hate for you to end up looking more of a fool.'

'More of a fool? Have you heard her Ken?'

'I heard her,' he said into his collar.

'Then blooming well say something!' Sheila reminded me of a Yorkshire terrier after a Hereford bull – all bluster. And her husband sat in his chair, out of his depth, and wary to touch his trifle.

Our Doris had that triumphant gleam in her eyes I hadn't seen since she got us upgraded to first class by claiming an allergy to the recycled air in economy. Apparently, her lungs are used to refinement in their oxygen. 'Please,' she said, 'I wouldn't wish to cause Ken any more unnecessary stress. I don't believe there's enough food onboard, should he become even more upset. And I can't see as he's going to start deep sea fishing.'

'Don't you think this all verges on bullying?'

'I suppose it does.'

Sheila folded her arms.

There's something very scary about a woman folding her arms. My mind cast back to when Aunt Fan caught me and Valerie Burton in the ginnel behind Snape's. Only, if I remember rightly, it were when she unfolded her arms my problems started. Maybe that is where my wariness of folded arms comes from; the memory of my ears ringing for a fortnight. Aunt Fan had hands like paving stones.

Sheila's hands are daintier. I don't doubt she could give Mr Miyagi a run for his money when crossed, but her hands reminded me of fine bone china. Royal Albert – that sort of thing.

She looked at our Doris and said to her, she said, 'I admit Ken shouldn't have said what he did about your headscarf, but that does not give you the right to be downright rude. This is a five star cruise liner, not a school changing room.'

After some consideration, our Doris said to Sheila, she said, 'Firstly, that was superbly put. I would have liked to use that line myself.'

This elicited something of the smile from Sheila.

Our Doris continued, 'Secondly, I apologise for any words that may have been construed as bullying. Quite honestly, when Ken told me my headscarf made me look like Lily Savage without the wig or attraction, I was offended. When he went on to question where I didn't indeed look like Mrs Overall, I realised how beneath me he is, and can only feel shame at sinking to his subterranean levels.'

The ire rose in Sheila again, her cheeks as pink as luncheon meat. She was all set to speak but our Doris hadn't finished. She said to her, she said, 'Your husband is a coward, and a bottom-feeder. He is such a parasite it's a wonder David Attenborough hasn't made a documentary about him yet.' She turned on Ken then, saying, 'You know this is true, you lazy, trifle-guzzling layabout. I hope beyond hope you see the error of your ways, because I feel sorry for the poor beggars who have to carry your coffin, or will Sheila be hiring a forklift?'

Silence.

This is what it took for Ken to put his trifle down. He set it on the bedside table and, meek as anything, murmured, 'You act as though I never exercise – just sit here eating all day.'

'You don't?'

Ken shook his head. He said to us, he said, 'We're training for a dance competition.'

Our Doris's eyes went wide. She looked every inch the electrocuted ostrich as she said to him, she said, 'One: dance can be a reputable form of exercise, whilst also being a classic pastime. Two: I hope you're sticking to a waltz, you've too much trifle in your veins for a paso doble. And, three: what dance competition is this?'

Sheila couldn't have looked more smug. 'It completely slipped my mind that you've never been on a cruise before, especially not one so stately. Anyhow, on each trip there is a dance competition. It's all very traditional. Everybody dresses up. I've had a gown made specially, by a local lad not impartial to a sequin.'

'And Ken? What will he be wearing?' Our Doris struggled to part her lips around the words, her teeth were clenched that tight. She were seething. I hadn't seen her so livid since Carry on Columbus, and even then she found a kind word for June Whitfield.

Once again, we found ourselves facing a smug Sheila. I couldn't blame her. We'd mocked her husband's physical health, and now she had the perfect opportunity to embarrass us whilst sharing news of his alternative exercise regime.

Sheila puffed out her chest, looking every inch the hen, and she said, all satisfied, she said, 'Ken got a bespoke suit crafted by the same tailor with accoutrements to match my gown.'

The cogs whirred in our Doris's head. I could practically see them whirring ten to the dozen in our Doris's head. She said to Sheila, she said, 'How lovely you have something to share – and hopefully is beneficial to Ken's heart.'

'I imagine it will be. Ken is regional champion after all.'

'Is that so?'

I must admit Sheila's smile got annoying. She was like some strange combination of Pennywise and the Cheshire Cat, using her smile to its fullest as she said, 'Oh yes, Ken danced professionally before his operation. Now, we stick to these *amateur* contests. You know, add a bit of celebrity to the occasion.'

Our Doris nodded. She managed to pull a smile from somewhere and plastered it to her face. Her cheeks almost cracked it was that forced. She faced Ken and said to him, she said, 'Please accept my most sincere apologies for our presumptions regarding your lifestyle. Indeed, it seems you put 'arold and myself to shame with such an active occupation. I can only imagine the effort it takes for you to maintain such a physique when you're clearly most adept in your field.'

The two of them grinned at our Doris, not understanding what she'd just said, lost in the rose-tinted idea they'd won.

Ken even went so far as to say, he said, 'That's all

right, Doris. Thanks for saying sorry. I admit, I do get a bit sensitive about my weight, but you would, too, if you'd been in my shoes.'

Sheila went on, 'It really is big of you to apologise on 'arold's behalf. I know how hard it is for a man to admit when he's wrong.'

I were all set to protest, give them the whole, 'now just a minute,' but our Doris took hold of my arm and steered me towards the door. She said to Sheila, 'Thank you for being so understanding. Hopefully, we can put this entire matter to rest, and our husbands will be drinking buddies once more.'

'We're training tonight, but I'm sure Ken would like nothing more. See you, Doris.'

With that, she closed the door on us.

Our Doris gripped my arm that hard on the way back to our cabin, her French manicure nearly broke the skin – it were like being held in the talon's of a giant eagle, like something out of *The Lord of the Rings*.

Safely locked away in our own quarters, I sat on the bed rubbing my arm. I said to our Doris, I said, 'What were that for, our Doris?'

She started her pacing as soon as we were through the door. She stopped and gave me the Look. This Look was something fierce. I didn't know what I'd done to achieve it, but it must have been bad, because our Doris was set to turn me to stone, a regular Medusa she was, and she said to me, she said, 'All I ever wanted was a husband who could display some modicum of tact, instead, I get you. Has anything I've said in the last fifty-six years sunk in, our 'arold? Or did something go missing from that ginormous head of yours – because that is the only reason I can imagine you would think it apt to offend a regional dance champion.'

'It was typical bloke's banter.'

'I'm sorry – are you a bloke, 'arold Copeland? Because I had it in my head that you were a upper middle-class gentleman with leanings towards Labour, not some gadless proletariat.'

'Gadless?'

'Yes, gadless. Don't start questioning my linguistics now, not when they've just pulled you out of a scrape worse than that time you were seen in the same car park as Eleanor Stockwell.'

I could have pulled my hair out there and then with little concern for the follicles. I said to her, I said, 'Nothing happened with Eleanor Stockwell. How many times do I have to tell you?'

'I know nothing happened with Eleanor Stockwell. You're not stupid enough to go in for anything extracurricular, but the mere societal implication was too much to bear.'

'I thought you were on my side. You were all for insulting Ken until you found out he likes to potter around a dance floor like a discount Anton du Beke.'

'Because I thought he was a layabout – a no-good fool with a penchant for lard. You gave me false information.'

'I didn't give you any information.'

'The one time I defend you and you go and offend someone with possible celebrity connections.'

'You're not supposed to care about that anymore. I thought you'd got over all that nonsense.'

'Nonsense? Nonsense? I've had aspirations my entire life, our 'arold, and just because I've realised it's an issue doesn't mean I'll give it up.'

'No. You're just worried what he'll tell these possible celebrity connections about Mrs Doris Copeland of Partridge Mews.'

'So, what if I am? Is that a crime?'

'It's not a crime but it's downright stupid.'

Then came the knock at the door. It shut our Doris up and she'd been on the verge of saying something completely venomous.

Our Doris, ever the hostess, went over and answered the door. It was Sheila, her smile in overdrive. I don't know how long she'd been listening, but she'd definitely heard enough. She said, by way of introduction, she said, 'Not interrupting anything, I hope.'

I didn't give our Doris chance to respond. I had this burst of inspiration bubbling in my chest like a soda stream. I looked Sheila dead in the eye and, imitating our Doris, I said to her, I said, 'On the contrary, we were simply discussing what dance we will perform in the competition. You will understand how heated the conversation can get when one wants to pull off a spectacular performance.

'The fact of the matter is that I haven't danced since my knee operation, and I was understandably concerned about attempting anything too frenetic.'

Sheila's smile slipped a bit when she said, 'You're entering the competition?'

'We used to dance all the time. Everyone did, but with modern pastimes taking hold, we only ever get to waltz on special occasions. This competition seemed the perfect opportunity to get our glad rags on and enjoy ourselves.'

Sheila gulped back her unease. 'Well that's really good to hear. I'm glad our disagreement inspired something fulfilling. I simply called to say as we've rearranged some things and Ken would be quite happy to go for a drink with you this evening.

'Sounds like a plan,' I said.

'Right well, I best be off.' And she scuttled away, faster than a silverfish under a skirting board.

Our Doris closed the door. She faced me, turning as slowly as anything so as I couldn't be sure whether I was about to be murdered or merely maimed.

She had a smile on her face, positively beaming, as she said to me, she said, 'That was a stroke of genius, our 'arold. Whilst I dispute the use of the term glad rags, I couldn't have said it better myself.'

'It's a good job our Theo's coming on board, he can help us with the routine.'

She nodded. 'I cannot imagine why I didn't know about the competition sooner. I'll have to speak to Veronica.'

'Does this mean you're my friend again, our Doris?'

'No, 'arold, it doesn't. I'm not your friend, I'm your wife.'

I can't pretend I wasn't disheartened. I said, 'Does being my wife mean you can't be my friend.'

'Listen to me, Harold Copeland. Alf is your friend. To some extent Percy is your friend. I should hope you don't do with them what you do with me.

I said to her, I said, 'And what's that?'

'Close the curtains and you'll find out.'

There it was: the bluebottle in my chest, that familiar blush to our Doris's cheeks as she locked the door.

I never anticipated getting up to mischief on the high seas, but we made mincemeat of those hospital corners.

A few days down the line, the ship docked in Lisbon.

When we first planned our trip, we knew we wanted to bring Theo along. Our Angela was the one who mentioned his GCSE's and asked us to wait until his summer holidays, otherwise I could envisage our Doris writing all manner of letters to various exam boards to see if it would be possible for him to be tested on a cruise ship. Instead, she has waited nearly two months for her only grandchild, the apple of her eye, to set foot on deck.

I knew she was excited. I hadn't figured on just how maniacally excited she could get.

The night before we were due to meet Theo, our Doris didn't sleep. Over our fifty-six years together I've grown impervious to her snoring. Though she sounds like a trombone with a melon trapped in its tubes, I can live with it.

Now we're on the ship, our Doris doesn't sleep. Insomnia has her in its clutches and we've no way of fixing it. Not that I want it fixing. I know it must be terrible for our Doris to miss all her dreams about perfectly organised doily displays, but I'm getting more sleep than I have done since marrying her.

When I last glimpsed her, before I slipped into a dream about Anthea Turner and sausage rolls, she had a smile on her face. A proper serial killer smile, as she stared off into space. She'd checked her itinerary twenty-two times to memorise it and sat like a toddler all set for her first trip to the zoo.

Next morning, our Doris was in the same position, only showered, dressed, and putting her earrings on – Marc Cain costume jewellery, expensive enough to leave an impression without looking like a flagrant display of consumerism.

I said to her, I said, 'Morning, our Doris.'

'Never you mind, "morning our Doris",' she said, 'get in the en-suite and make yourself presentable, our 'arold. The boat docks in two hours and I refuse to leave our Theo waiting on a foreign pier like some Victorian orphan.'

'We're in Portugal.'

'Exactly. Foreign. There's too much sangria in their veins to be truly punctual.'

I went and got ready, leaving our Doris to fritter away over her handbag. There's no use talking to our Doris when she's frittering over her handbag.

Eventually, the boat docked – on time.

The sun was out, and our Doris finally allowed me to wear flip-flops; they're designer and our Doris will let me have anything if it's designer, says as it's a relief to have a husband with fashionable interests.

Our Doris stood as close to the guard-rail as she could without taking a dip in the drink. She were like a spaniel searching for a tennis ball as she scanned the dock for our Theo. In fact, I felt this tension build in my chest that if they didn't let us off soon she would throw herself from the deck, all Kate Winslet in Titanic, she was that eager to find our grandson.

I said to her, I said, 'You'll give yourself a coronary in a minute, our Doris.'

She stepped back to give me the Look and said to me, she said, 'Please find a less cliché warning, our 'arold. You ought to know my heart is in perfect health. One cannot hold an afternoon tea for a few dozen octogenarians with the threat of heart failure.'

I nodded as she went back to her scrutinising of the dock. I admit I were excited at the prospect of seeing our Theo. I'd have been happy to see anyone from home, honestly, but I wasn't about to launch myself from the boat to meet them.

I understand it really.

Our Doris and Theo have been as close as curtains since his birth. She has sculpted that lad into the perfect Stepford teenage boy of every grandmother's dreams. And she hadn't seen him for two months. She looked set to tear the ship apart with her bare hands if they didn't let the gangplank down soon.

They finally let us off the boat. When she caught sight of Theo, our Doris was fit to scream, ready to wail worse than when I took her to see Cliff Richard in nineteen-seventy-four.

Theo sauntered over to us, a smile on his face, as composed as a panther along a branch. He'd caught something of a tan, had clearly dressed himself according to our Doris's rules of civility.

Not that our Doris recalled them in that moment. She ran towards him, arms outstretched, linen jacket spreading behind her like dragon wings.

Theo's eyes widened that much it were a wonder they didn't fall out their sockets and roll like marbles. He braced himself for impact as our Doris rocketed into him, practically knocking all the air from his lungs. It's a good job he isn't asthmatic.

It were definitely a sight to be seen. Our Doris has been against overt displays of affection since nineteen-sixty-two when I gave her a peck on the cheek at Bill Newton's wedding. I don't think anyone noticed because they were all focused on the grass stains on his Norma's dress, but our Doris couldn't have it getting around that her husband tried to steal the bride's limelight.

She looked as though she'd been trained by a python, she hugged our Theo that tightly.

He was as uncomfortable as you'd imagine a sixteen-year-old boy to look when he's being mauled by his Nan in a foreign country.

I took the time our Doris spent hugging Theo to get a proper look at him because lord had he grown.

He was tall before, but now he stood at least a foot taller than our Doris.

He still looked shocked as anything at being embraced with such force. At first, he stood with his arms at his sides, face contorted in such a way you'd be forgiven for thinking he were being attacked. He slowly wrapped his arms around his grandmother, a slim, uncertain smile settling on his face. He said to our Doris, he said, 'It's good to see you too, Nan.' He attempted to extricate himself from her clutches, but our Doris were having none of it.

I stood with my hands in my pockets as folk milled about around us, all of them keen to explore the city whilst a crazed older lady performed some strange approximation of the Heimlich manoeuvre on a young man.

I said to our Theo, I said, ''ow at, Theo?'

He chuckled. His laugh had gained more depth, sounding as masculine as an axle grinder, and I found myself aware of how old I'd got. He said to me, he said, 'I'm fine, Grandad. At least I was before Nan assaulted me.'

Our Doris sniffed as loud as a hedgehog with a head cold. She'd kept her face hidden for the majority of the hug and it was only as she slurped back the snot that we realised she were crying.

I said to her, 'Are you all right, love?'

She wheezed, trying to calm herself, before saying, 'Of course I'm all right, our 'arold. I'm just the slightest bit emotional. It is allowed you know?'

I stared Theo dead in the eye. 'That's me told.'

There isn't much a person can do when our Doris finds her emotions. I reached for her shoulder. 'Let's go find a coffee,' I said.

'Are you sure she doesn't need something stronger?'

I shook my head. Our Doris's neck snapped back. She stared at Theo with a grim set to her jaw, ever the gargoyle as she said to him, she said, 'Whilst I understand alcohol being used in plenty of situations, my grandson should not. Nor do I appreciate the suggestion that it takes alcohol for me to gain some appearance of sensibility. Besides, is it completely wrong for a person to miss their grandchild?'

'Coffee it is then,' Theo said, finally tearing himself away from our Doris. 'Since you missed me so much you can pay.'

We weren't long searching for a coffee shop. Rather than let either of them talk about ambience, or décor, I led them into the first place we came across, left them in a window seat and went to order.

The server looked like a cross between Brunhilda and Catherine Zeta-Jones. She had broad shoulders, dark hair, and this face that could have belonged to a warthog. I'd never thought I'd be attracted to Mervyn Davies in drag, but as I approached the counter, I felt the familiar flutter in my chest I get when I watch my Charlie Dimmock videos. It were either that, or indigestion.

I immediately forgot all the Portuguese our Doris had me learn. Before we reach any new country, she has me study the basic elements of their language because she refuses to have us seen as ignorant British plebs.

It had already got me into trouble once when I went to order a bowl of rice in Phuket and ended up with a bowl of crickets.

I had to summon some of my new language skills as

I approached the server. I said to her, I said, 'Konnichiwa, trois café latte, sil vous favore.'

She shook her head. 'English?' she asked, and I realised what it meant to be an ignorant British pleb.

I nodded.

'What can I do you for?' It was in that moment I recognised her accent. I must have looked a bit shell-shocked because she said to me, she said, 'I'm from Bolton.'

I mumbled as I said, 'Can I get three lattes please?'

She nodded. 'There's no need to look so glum, you weren't to know I'm one of your own.'

'I did try and learn the lingo.'

'You don't have to convince me, duck, folk don't even bother to learn gracias.'

'Isn't that Spanish?'

'See what I mean?'

I paid for the coffees and carried them to the table.

'Did you use your Portuguese?' our Doris said.

'I tried.'

'That's something at least.' Our Doris took her latte and stirred the foam away before saying, 'It's a good job we're on the continent, there's no way I could make such a flagrant display of gluttony in an English coffee shop.'

'Cappuccinos have the same amount of milk, Nan.'

'Really?' Our Doris looked at Theo, gone out. A smile bloomed on her face. 'That certainly changes things.'

Before she could continue and tell us all about the social consequences of consuming too much milk in public, I said to Theo, I said, 'How did the exams go?'

He came over all melancholy. A shadow settled over his face like Ann Widdecombe in front of a vending machine. He said to us, he said, 'Without my grandparents around to guide me, I could not muster the requisite mental strength to attend. Instead, I spent my days lingering outside off-licenses waiting for disreputable old people to go past who I'd ask to buy me cheap cider and cigarettes. I became close friends with Janice Dooley of Little Street.'

My heart fell into my stomach. I glanced from Theo to our Doris, whose face had fallen – her jowls as sad as bulldogs. She looked all set to cry again.

Until Theo burst out laughing. The guffaws came straight from the stomach. He clapped his hands on the table, which ever one of us he looked at sent him further into a fit of hysteria. 'You should see your faces,' he said, 'Lord, you're important to me, but I didn't miss you enough to throw my life away. Do you honestly believe Mum would let me come on this trip if I did that?'

Our Doris must have missed him more than I thought. She didn't give him the Look, she merely sipped her drink and said, 'That was a very cruel trick to play, our Theo. Though I appreciate a good joke as much as the next person, the very idea that you could become associated with Janice Dooley of Little Street is the stuff of nightmares.'

He said, 'You don't have to worry about that, Nan. If I were going to ask anyone for a beer, I'd ask Alf.'

She turned on me like something out of The Exorcist, the Look as demonic as ever. 'Have you heard him, our 'arold? Your friendship with Alfred Simpson has our grandson headed towards teenage alcoholism.'

'It's a good job I'm coming on this boat then. Keep me out of trouble.'

I couldn't help myself, I said, 'Thanks Theo.'

He beamed at me, raising his glass. 'Don't mention it, Grandad.'

We chose to wait until we were back on the boat before telling Theo about the dance competition. It was too risky on land. Undoubtedly, he'd have us practising our stretches in the Praça do Comércio.

I haven't danced with our Doris in years. Since Theo first developed an interest in dancing – I regret to this day letting him watch Strictly Come Dancing – he's been her first choice of partner. I'm not fussed really, but there's a certain trepidation of being upstaged by my grandson, and I wasn't prepared for that to happen when we were admiring souvenir cockerels in a foreign country.

Our Doris doesn't tend to go in for souvenirs, but our Theo said as there's a tackiness with some items that suits certain millennial ideals whilst also celebrating the Portuguese culture. I tell you, whenever that boy starts on about social ideals, I fear for the future.

I question whether I had such confidence at his age, feeling I knew the way the world worked, or whether I were more concerned about who I'd take dancing down the pavilion on a Saturday. Our Doris might have been my first major girlfriend, but a lot of that was to do with the inevitable fretting that came with having to find someone to dance with down the pavilion on a Saturday.

Our Theo got his own cabin. When we booked the trip, we knew that no matter how much we missed him, we categorically did not want to share a cabin with a teenager. There's too many hormones.

Before we settled though, we had to tell him about the competition. Despite wanting to sample a real Portuguese feast in a proper eatery, the boat was leaving early in the evening, meaning we had to settle for a complimentary glass of sangria on board.

We sat at our table awaiting our food, only for Mrs Veronica Ambrose to appear, casting a shadow like our very own Empire State Building. She paired a large red straw hat with tonight's outfit. Our Doris says as Veronica has an outfit for every occasion, I said I didn't realise there were so many varieties of tent. This was another of those times I got in trouble for being fatphobic.

Our Doris made the introductions.

Veronica said to our Theo, she said, 'Good evening, Theodore, your grandmother has told me a great many things about you.'

Theo conjured his best gentlemanly smile, all Twyford's-bright teeth, and a glimmer in his eyes, giving him a look of the Cheshire Cat after a trip to the dental hygienist. He said to Veronica, he said, 'I hope they were all quite horrible. I must say you're quite the elusive creature. Last I heard, my dear grandmother was trying to solve the mystery of your identity.'

'I wouldn't quite put it like that,' said our Doris.

'You can't deny it, Nan. You treated Mrs Ambrose like the ship's very own mermaid.'

He impressed Veronica in any case, she stood at the head of the table and tittered. She honestly tittered, like a schoolgirl mooning over her science teacher. She said to him, she said, 'Doris wasn't joking when she told me you were well-spoken. I must confess I hadn't quite believed a young man capable of such eloquence.'

'You flatter me. Will you be joining us for dinner, Mrs Ambrose?'

'I do have my own table received,' she said, her protests feeble, and polite, the very essence of being British.

If anything, this spurred Theo on. He said to her, he said, 'Please do accept my invitation, Mrs Ambrose. I should like nothing more than to dine with the closest acquaintance my Nan has made on this cruise.'

'You've twisted my arm,' she said, as fast as a whippet down a zipwire. 'It shouldn't matter anyway tonight. The chef is treating us all to Portuguese-inspired three course meal.'

'That would be most welcome. After a day of sight-seeing, we didn't get chance to sample the cuisine.'

'Dial it down a bit, Theo,' I said.

Our Doris fired the Look in my direction. 'Our grandson is simply expressing his joy at experiencing a luxury cruise for the first time. You'd do well to follow his example.'

'Expressing joy sounds a lot like simpering to me.' I necked a fair amount of my bitter. Our Doris doesn't like it when I drink alcohol like I'm dying of thirst, but there's a certain amount of satisfaction comes from a cool drink of bitter hitting the back of your throat. She's never understood it herself, but then I've never understood why she needs forty pairs of court shoes in assorted shades.

Veronica wasn't paying attention to us. She sat with her hand raised, staring daggers at one of the cruise staff. Not that they noticed. The brim of her hat cast such a shadow over her face, she looked as though she was nothing more than a chin. Eventually, they came over and she ordered herself a drink. I'd never thought her the type of person to enjoy a tequila sunrise.

Once we'd eaten our food – I remained silent for much of the meal, leaving our Doris, Theo and Veronica to get on with talking about the delicate balance of fish and rice, and how it leant itself quite nicely to the sangria – we decided it was time to tell Theo about the dance competition. At least, I eyed up our Doris and she gave this slight nod of her head. We were all set to speak up, when who should appear but Ken and Sheila.

Theo must have noticed the mood change because he immediately shut his mouth.

It might have also had something to do with the set of our Doris's shoulders. They pressed that hard into the back of her chair, it was a wonder the wood didn't crack. Her lips disappeared – leaving nothing more than a thin crease, some new wrinkle.

Even Veronica turned around to see just what had our Doris looking so vehement.

Sheila was the first to speak. She said to us, she said, 'I hadn't realised your grandson would be joining us on the trip so soon, Mr and Mrs Copeland. I thought it only right that we come over and introduce ourselves.'

Our Doris rapped her fingers along the table, seemingly to straighten the cloth, in actual fact I knew from experience that she was imagining thumping Sheila. She said to her, she said, 'If only I had been so civil. I must say I have monopolised my grandson's time today – it having been so long since last we spoke, I didn't consider introducing him to all and sundry.'

Veronica turned her chair around, giving herself a better look at Sheila and Ken – I swear, even her eyes widened at the sight of his gut. She said to Sheila, she said, 'I don't recall us having the pleasure of knowing one another, I'm Mrs Veronica Ambrose, and you are?'

Sheila accepted Veronica's outstretched hand with something akin to trepidation. I didn't blame her – Veronica did have a look of the rhinoceros about her. She said to her, she said, 'I'm Sheila, and this is my husband Ken. We're acquaintances of the Copelands.'

'Yes. That does seem the tiniest bit obvious considering we are all at their table.' She shifted her hat slightly and looked Sheila dead in the eye.

'All right, Ken?' I said.

He nodded. 'All right, 'arold?'

'What did you think to the paella? Probably a bit much after all that trifle, I should imagine.'

His smile made him look like a corpse, all gritted teeth and wandering eyes. He gave something of the chuckle, and said, 'I haven't had much by way of food today. We've been practising.'

'Yes, all right, Ken. There's no need to give away our each and every secret,' Sheila said, before going on to no one in particular, 'I can only imagine what it would be like if we brought our grandchildren on the ship – absolute mayhem, I should think. There's just too much of a threat of cabin fever for me to bring a teenager on board.'

Our Doris's lip twitched like a dog set to snarl.

It was our Theo who spoke up. He can be quick can our Theo when he's primed and ready. He said to Sheila, he said, 'Perhaps you underestimate the mindset of the modern teenager, ma'am. I don't blame you. So often in contemporary media we see the idea perpetuated that the young are louts leaving broken bottles in children's playgrounds and engaging in disreputable activities the world over. If we are to believe everything we see on screen then we undoubtedly forget to acknowledge the world around us and see just what our young are getting up to.

'I think you'll find that the ship has quite a considerable amount of groups and amenities to cater for the under-eighteens, but I can't think you will have checked, seeing as you couldn't possibly bring your grandchildren on this boat. Maybe they're part of the stereotypical group of youths I've just mentioned, with little respect for authority.

'I must admit this trip is something of the expense. That's one of the reasons my grandparents are only bringing me along for the final portion of the trip. We must all be somewhat more thrifty nowadays, mustn't we?'

My mouth dropped. I stared at our Theo as if stunned. It were like being sat across from a miniature Doris, only taller and more masculine. Even our Doris looked astounded and she's tried to avoid that since Niamh Kavanagh won Eurovision.

She never did forgive Ireland for that.

Sheila grimaced. She looked to be pained physically from our Theo's words. Her chest swallowed her throat, and her chin settled somewhere in her cleavage. Not that I'd ever admit to noticing another woman's cleavage in front of our Doris, but her chin definitely burrowed between her breasts like a dormouse in a hedgerow.

She said to our Doris, she said, 'It must fill you with a great sense of pride to have a grandson who takes after you, almost to a fault.'

'On the contrary, Sheila,' our Doris said, 'Theodore is his own person entirely. He has much more tact than me, I'm likely to tell an interfering busybody to buzz off.'

Veronica slurped her fourth tequila sunrise as she watched their exchange.

Ken stood, uncertain as ever, behind Sheila. He said to Sheila, he said, 'Maybe we should go back to the cabin, dear. It's been a long day.'

'It is so difficult when one must admit their infirmities.' Our Doris offered a smile and reached for her sauvignon blanc. She swilled it around her glass, eyes on the beads of condensation sidling down the stem, making a point not to look in Sheila's direction, ever the store manager dismissing their assistant.

Sheila smirked. 'You're one to talk of infirmities, Doris. You two can't even decide on a routine you're that worried about all your infirm parts.'

I saw something like intrigue flash through our Theo's eyes, but he kept quiet.

Our Doris looked set to use her wine as a weapon. She glowered at Sheila, giving her the full force of her Look, and said to her, she said, 'My apologies if my words caused offence. Once again, I demonstrate that I have grown somewhat tactless, but that can happen when one reaches such an age. I'm simply unwilling to contend with bovine muck.'

Veronica sniggered into her glass.

'We're not going through this again, our Doris. We've been arguing with them for that long I'm beginning to think we're in an episode of Eastenders.' I supped my bitter before saying to Theo, I said, 'There's a dance competition, our Theo. Your Nan and me are going to enter and we thought you could help us with the routine. What do you say?'

I have to say it warmed my heart to bring such a grin to our Theo's face. He didn't speak to me though, no, he directed his words in Sheila's direction. He said to her, he said, 'When is it?'

That's when me and our Doris realised the detail we'd overlooked. We met each other's gazes as it dawned on us that we'd no idea how long we had to train. I sat their envisaging the crew pushing back our tables and chairs, declaring tonight's the night.

Veronica brought us back down to earth saying, she said, 'It's not for a fortnight. Once we've had our big final night of entertainment – hosted by premier Blackpool drag queen Betty Fiddles – the floor is opened up for couples to compete.' She downed the last half of her drink and ordered another.

'And do the couples all dance her in the dining hall?' Our Theo had the questions we should have asked earlier.

'Oh no, dear. We've rather a splendid ballroom. I can ask someone to let you take a look, if you like, really get a feel for the place.'

'It would be an honour if you could give me the tour yourself, Mrs Ambrose. If it isn't too much trouble.'

She tittered again, and I worried for whoever found themselves under the spell of our Theo's charm.

Veronica's tittering was cut short by Sheila saying, she said, 'You never offered us a tour of the ballroom.'

'That's because I don't like you,' Veronica said. Clearly, inebriation agreed with her.

Sheila's cheeks ballooned in fury. She looked set to speak her mind, but once more our Theo chose to defuse the situation, he said to her, he said, 'Will you be entering the competition?'

'I'm regional champion,' Ken stammered.

Sheila stood, arms crossed, tongue pressed against the back of her teeth, so she looked like a cross between a prison inmate and a bulldog. She said nothing.

Our Theo, meanwhile, said to Ken, he said, 'That's quite the achievement. What region?'

'Don't tell him,' Sheila hissed.

'I can't tell you.'

'All right,' said Theo, 'I merely wished to congratulate you, and look forward to seeing your dancing skills.'

'I imagine you're some sort of professional.' Sheila did a good job at being perpetually grumpy. I'm not sure her face could handle any sort of happy emotion.

Our Theo shook his head. He shared a smile Colgate would be proud of and said to her, he said, 'Whilst I do have something of the education, and have trodden the boards a few times, I would not like to call myself a professional. It may leave a bitter taste in the mouths of those who've spent their lives cultivating a career for themselves in the industry.'

'My Ken has taught the artform for decades.'

'Well you know what they say about those who can't.' Theo's words immediately put paid to our Doris's ideas about him having tact. Either way, watching Sheila and Ken scuttle off, we all of us laughed like schoolchildren on too many bonbons.

Next morning, I wasn't laughing.

It couldn't have been much past dawn when I found myself awoken by an overly enthusiastic Theo nearly knocking the door down in his excitement.

Our Doris lumbered out of bed. She's not too spry at five o'clock in the morning is our Doris, especially after a few too many glasses of sangria.

The door had barely opened when our Theo burst into the room, bouncing across the room on the balls of his feet. He stopped at the end of the bed, eyes adjusting to the semi-darkness. A glance around the room told him all he needed to know. 'You're not ready,' he said, an air of disappointment to his tone. He sagged down slightly, not quite a slouch – I'm not sure he'd ever dare slouch in front of our Doris – but enough that I could see every hint of disappointment in his bone structure.

Our Doris let the door click shut. She turned around, the wiry tufts of hair as close to disarray as they could get – not quite a tumbleweed but she wouldn't look amiss in The Good, the Bad, and the Ugly. When she spoke, her words were filled with the gritty burr of a bear woken from hibernation; she said to him, she said, 'I hadn't realised you intended for us to start training so early, our Theo.'

'What about the early bird and all that?'

'What are you talking about?' she said, leaning against the wall.

'You,' he said, 'you're always going on about the early bird catching the worm.'

Our Doris let out a small grunt that could have been a snore. Her eyes were closed entirely as she staggered back towards the bed. She said to him, slipping back beneath the covers, she said, 'That's for when we're on land. There's too much water for any birds to even think about catching a worm.'

'We're not training yet, then?' There was no bounce in his steps now.

I said to him, I said, 'How about we start when it's actually light out?'

He headed back towards the door. 'I'll be back at eight. We can have breakfast, but then we're training, and I'll accept no excuses.'

Three hours later we met him in the dining hall. He sat at our table with Percy. When we approached, they were deep in conversation about the benefits of blueberries. Our Theo finished and said, 'You finally chose to wake up then?'

Our Doris gave him a subdued version of the Look and said to him, she said, 'Whilst you may find it humorous to mock us for not awakening at the crack of dawn, I will remind you that you're that renowned for slumbering till lunchtime, we spent the best part of a year worrying you were a narcoleptic.'

Percy and I went to order breakfast. As we waited in line, he said to me, he said, 'That grandson of yours is certainly a character, isn't he?'

'What did he do now?'

'He joined me for my morning run.'

'You look as shocked as I am,' I said.

'Nobody joins me on my morning run.'

'He's changed a lot in two months.'

We placed our orders and went back to the table.

Percy wasn't too keen on me ordering three Full English breakfasts, but that didn't stop him from ordering four sausages, two rashers of bacon, and five fried eggs. He said it was for the protein content, but I couldn't help but question whether being so long on the boat had started to impact him for the positive.

After breakfast, our Theo had us assemble on deck, and I regretted our meal immediately. He revealed just why he'd been running with Percy – because our grandson, the teenager we had missed for near eleven weeks, expected us to run with him.

I said to him, I said, 'You do know that I have a new knee, our Theo?'

'You got that knee six years ago, Grandad.' He was stretching at the time, paying barely any attention to me.

'Your Nan only got her hip last year.'

'She was running a few months later.'

Our Doris gave me the Look and said to me, she said, 'Leave him be, our 'arold. It'll be good for us both to get a bit of exercise in. We might have been calling Ken, but you have to admit we're both of us getting a touch out of shape.'

I wasn't about to disagree with our Doris, so I said to her, I said, 'All right then, our Doris, let's get some running done then.'

Now I can't say as I've done much running since I retired. Sure, I go and meander around the countryside. I've even been known to take a trip down the canal towpath every once in a while, but as far as I'm concerned running went out with Bruce's Price is Right.

Adequately warmed up, we ran. Well our Theo ran. Me and our Doris lagged along behind him, unable to run more than half the deck before our faces were luncheon meat. I couldn't speak for her, but my heart were beating faster than Ringo Starr.

The worst part was that our Theo wasn't even going fast. He slowed himself down to suit the pace of his septuagenarian grandparents, more of a jog than a sprint, and yet we still couldn't keep up with him.

He had us running the entire length and breadth of the ship – abovedeck, below deck. We ran past all of our acquaintances, with our Doris stopping to wheeze a few words about how our Theo was her grandson and they were joining him for a light morning constitutional to celebrate our reunion. Meanwhile, me and Theo kept running.

A mere ninety minutes later, we finished our run.

We made him stop in the bar. I bought him half a lager, the best sort of hush money – I told our Doris it was shandy, in any case. My pint of bitter nearly didn't make it to the table, I'd drank that much beforehand. I know I should have water with me when I'm exercising, but I never anticipated that my grandson would try to off me by having me run to the point that my lungs felt like two hot air balloons crammed tight behind my ribcage.

I said to him, I said, 'Was there really a need to run, our Theo? It's a dance competition not a marathon.'

He tipped his glass in my direction, and said to me,

he said, 'You need to get that heart rate up, Grandad. For all you know, I'll have you dancing the Argentine tango.'

He didn't.

Once our drinks were drunk and we were looking less like three overboiled beetroots, our Theo led us to the ballroom, or some approximation of a ballroom, I'm more than certain that your everyday ballroom doesn't have a life-raft attached to the ceiling by a series of nets. An oversized glitterball hung from the ceiling like a forgotten globe of tinfoil.

Our Theo stood beneath the glitterball, eyeing us with a mixture of glee and scholarly trepidation. It were a look I hadn't seen since nineteen-fifty-two when sir let me loose with a Bunsen burner. He said to us, he said, 'Since you've a few ailments, I thought it best if we went with something slow. Do you remember the routine we did for the WI Christmas party?'

I said to him, I said, 'Which one?'

'We have done quite a few.' Our Doris offered Theo something that was supposed to be a smile.

'We'll be doing the Viennese waltz to "All of You" by John Legend.'

'And who's he when he's at home?'

Our Theo gave me a Look to rival his grandmother's, and said to me, he said, 'It's one of the most popular love songs of the last few years, has been certified platinum I don't know how many times, and has been used as almost every first dance at weddings since two-thousand-and thirteen, second only to Ed Sheeran's "Thinking out Loud".' His cheeks were red from his outburst. I found myself reminded of him as a toddler refusing to use the potty – there's something downright demonic about our Theo's face when he's wound up.

Our Doris was sympathetic. She looked at him all doleful, like a nun over a cheese sandwich, and she said to him, she said, 'Whilst it may be a lovely song, it's not something that suits me and your grandfather. I know I am renowned for my knowledge of modern pop music, but I cannot say the same for him. Therefore, may I suggest we choose a more suitable, classic song?'

'I planned an entire routine, Nan. Will you at least watch it once with the song I suggested?'

We agreed and he got on with it. He scrolled through his iPhone. Once the song started, he began his dance. He could have asked our Doris to dance with him so as it didn't look awkward, but I suppose we'd offended him enough for one day.

It wasn't a bad bit of dancing from what I could tell. He had the steady rise and fall, a few dips, nothing too difficult and a smile on his face, but none of it really spoke to me.

I said to him, I said, 'I can't see myself doing any of that, our Theo.'

His shoulders slumped, downtrodden. He said to me, he said, 'You don't want to dance at all, do you?'

Our Doris gave me the Look, the proper one, the one where you worry the gates of Hell will open at your feet and swallow you whole. She said to our Theo, she said, 'Of course he wants to dance. I believe you've come up with a beautiful routine, and the song does have a touch of the romantic about it. However, I'd prefer if we performed something closer to our waltz last Christmas. Perhaps to a tune by Mantovani – you know I've always liked his music. He has such a gentle way about him.'

'I'll see what I can do,' he said in that dismissive way

made famous by grandchildren the world over.

We'd upset him. He made no secret that we'd upset him.

I realised how much we'd upset him when he had us practising our spins. He did not care that I am a seventy-six-year-old man of Northern origin, he wanted to see me pirouette.

We didn't learn our dance that day.

Next day, we reconvened in the ballroom to discover that our Theo had brought along a guest. Mrs Veronica Ambrose stood beside him in her finest sportswear, an oxymoron in human form if ever there was one. She also wore dance shoes. I'd only seen her dancing once before and even then, she was no Ginger Rogers.

She beamed at our Doris as we entered and said to her, she said, 'I hope you don't mind but Theo here asked me to help prepare a new routine for you both, since he thought I'd have some knowledge about the sort of thing you'd like.'

'That is considerate,' our Doris said, jaw clenched.

'You're not entering the competition then?'

Veronica shook her head. 'Since I own the ship, I didn't think it appropriate that I enter the competition I funded. Besides, the prize is a plaster of Paris trophy I found on a market stall when we went to Bangkok – I'm not too fussed about winning.'

They got on with dancing. At least the song was more suitable. 'I wasn't able to find any Mantovani,' our

Theo said. He'd done something different today and the music started playing through the ballroom's speakers.

I looked to our Doris, she looked back at me, as Elvis Presley sang his "Love me Tender" across the ballroom.

We watched our Theo and Veronica waltz. It was already much better than what he'd shown us the day before. Our Theo stood a head above Veronica, and despite my preconceptions about her, she could move with the best of them. She had all the grace of a hippopotamus as our Theo led her about the ballroom. They had rhythm.

My spine chilled, and gooseflesh spread up my arms, and I felt as giddy as the first time I caught sight of a bit more than just ankle.

Our Theo had outdone himself.

I smiled across at our Doris. She stood with her hands clasped in front of her, as though in prayer, her eyes glittered, and she were beaming. Although whenever our Theo does something particularly triumphant her eyes glitter. She wouldn't have made it through his nursery graduation without half a ton of Kleenex.

When they finished our Theo looked at us, all hopeful. He said to us, he said, 'Well?'

I looked to our Doris, as speechless as when Mrs Cribbins brought guacamole to a primary school fundraiser in nineteen-eighty-eight. I said to him, I said, 'I think we're on to a winner, our Theo.'

His grin matched his grandmother's. 'Shall we start training?'

We did.

Veronica didn't bother sticking around. She claimed

a prior commitment, but there were a sheen of sweat on her brow that made her look as though she were on the verge of a pulmonary embolism, or in desperate need of a toilet.

Our Theo was keen on having us warm up properly before letting us get on with the dancing. He'd been looking on the internet and discovered some limbering exercises for the over-fifties. I pointed out my fifties were long since past but he were having none of it, and our Doris were keen to get started.

I stretched parts of my body I didn't know could stretch. There were this twinge in my spine; I hadn't thought it possible for a bone to feel like an elastic band being thwacked against a table but that's what happened. According to our Theo this was perfectly normal for someone not used to regular exercise.

After the stretching came the star jumps, and the jogging on the spot, before eventually we got around to any dancing.

We spent the best part of six hours training.

Our Theo homed in on getting us to get our hand placement correct. It turns out I've been holding our Doris wrong for more than half a century. She was as smug as Ethel's Willy in Eastenders when he went and stole that Christmas turkey. Until our Theo pointed out that she kept trying to lead.

She said to him, she said, 'And why shouldn't I lead?'

'Because you want to win the competition.'

She acknowledged he was right with a grimace and allowed me the chance to lead her around the ballroom.

After all our training, and a spot of late lunch, I disappeared to the bar for a drink.

Percy was already there, supping a lime and soda. I ordered a pint of bitter and went to join him.

He said to me, he said, 'How's things, Harry?'

I exhaled, practically deflating, as I sat down.

'I think our Theo's trying to kill me.'

Percy laughed. He howled at me the way you'd expect a fitness freak to howl at an out of shape septuagenarian.

Whilst he chortled, I glugged back my bitter. I won't lie. I was definitely trying to choke back my embarrassment.

He said to me, he said, 'I'm sorry, but it's only a bit of dancing.'

'It's not just a bit of dancing, though. Twice he's had us running throughout the entire flaming ship. That's your fault by the way. He only came on your morning run to find out how to properly torture his grandparents.'

'You could do with a bit of a run, Harry.'

'A bit of a run? A bit of a run? I wouldn't mind a bit of a run. He has us doing a bleeding marathon.'

'It's been two days.'

'And that's two days too many.'

'I knew you had a touch of laziness about you, but I didn't have you down as a couch potato.'

'I'm not as bad as Ken.'

Percy rolled his eyes. 'Right,' he said.

We sat silent for a few minutes. Honestly, he'd given me food for thought. It isn't that I mind exercise – our Doris wouldn't like it getting around that her husband leads a life of inactivity because he doesn't have enough to be getting on with in his retirement – but there is a sense of going through the motions on a cruise. I get up, wander around deck, watch a bit of telly in the cabin, have a few drinks in the bar, go to bed. If we stop off in a country then we do a bit of wandering about the place, seeing the sights. Our Doris has me taking photographs on the iPad – she brings along a variety of headscarves so as she doesn't clash with any of the backdrops she chooses – and before we know it, it's time to return to the boat.

It could be a bit of cabin fever.

It could be boredom.

I must admit that when we booked to go on a three month around the world cruise, I hadn't expected to spend so much time at sea. I read Jules Verne as a lad, I know a thing or two about travelling the globe at speed.

After mulling over my bitter for a bit, I said to Percy, I said, 'I think I've been on this boat too long.'

'Getting a bit homesick?'

I nodded. 'We did this trip for our Doris, but I think we'd have been better off with two weeks in Prestatyn.'

'Let me get this straight, Harry. Rather than see the entirety of the world on a luxury cruise liner, enjoying all the amenities man has to offer, you would have preferred to spend your time getting rained on in a Welsh seaside town?'

'I suppose.'

'And all of this because your grandson's helping train you for a dance competition?'

'It sounds stupid when you put it like that,' I said.

'That's because it is stupid. You're seventy-six, healthy for the most part, and privileged enough that you didn't have to worry about the cost of this trip. You've also managed to maintain something of the healthy relationship with your Theo – my daughter didn't say two words to me during puberty.'

'What're you getting at, Percy?' I asked. Half my pint had disappeared and I were itching to get another one. Lord, does dancing give me a dry throat.

He said to me, Percy said, 'I'm not getting at anything, Harry, I'm simply trying to give you some perspective – you'd do well to come along to one of the mindfulness sessions.'

'I've said it once, and I'll say it again, when you live with our Doris for as long as I have, you learn a thing or two about mindfulness.'

We had a few more drinks before Percy disappeared. Apparently, he'd had one lime and soda too many and would pay for it on the treadmill. I left him to it and went in search of our Theo. We'd invited him on this trip, and I sure as damn it was going to spend at least some time with him.

Next morning, I couldn't move.

I woke up, tried to stand and was hit by a bolt of lightning in my lower back. I thought this is it, our Doris has finally invested in a taser and you're going to feel her wrath for accidentally breaking part of her Portmeirion dinner set in nineteen-eighty-four. Only this weren't our Doris. She were still snoring in the bed, completely oblivious to the fact that her husband was enduring pain he hadn't felt since his knee operation.

I needed to get out of bed, if only to use the facilities, but my back were having none of it. Every movement came with a great jolt that felt as though my spine were being shattered beneath a sledgehammer.

I must have made too much noise, because no sooner had I considered wetting myself and claiming incontinence, than our Doris were telling me off, she said to me, she said, 'All this writhing better not mean you're up to mischief, our 'arold.'

I said to her, unsure how I managed to speak, I said, 'I can't move, our Doris.'

I felt sure she were giving me the Look. I couldn't see her because I was facing the other way contemplating the curtains, but there were the ominous silence that comes with the Look. 'I should have known you'd try something like this.'

Sweat beaded on my brow, worse than any gym session. 'I'm not trying anything, I can't bleeding move.'

I have to give it to our Doris, there were something like concern when she next spoke, saying to me, she said, 'Why can't you move?'

'It's my back,' I said, 'I've done my back in.'

Just saying the words brought tears to my eyes. I was glad for the near dark of a curtained cabin because no man wants to be seen with tears in his eyes if there hasn't been a major death in the family, or it isn't to do with football. Almost any emotion is allowed when it comes to football, especially tears. I once saw a seventeen stone bodybuilder reduced to tears when Wayne Rooney fractured his metatarsal.

Concern bloomed on our Doris's face, something that doesn't happen often because she likes to say she has the bedside manner of a nineteen-fifties ward matron, emotionless in the face of brutality. She said to me, she said, 'I think I best go and get the doctor.'

I nodded, pressing my face into the pillow, and said to her, I said, 'If they can't come just smother me.'

She said, 'I've had plenty of opportunity in the last fifty-six years, our 'arold, and I'm beggared if I kill you with a pillow that isn't my own.' With that she scuttled out of the cabin.

I could tell she were worried because she left in her bedclothes, and she prays as a woman's bedclothes should only be viewed by her husband and some close personal friends who may accompany them on a couples' retreat. We've never been on a couples' retreat, but she's been a fan of the idea since she saw Summer Holiday.

Our Doris brought the doctor back with her. There's nothing quite like a doctor for making me feel ancient. It doesn't matter whether they're twenty-five or fifty-five, they all come with this air of disappointment about them at having to deal with the ailments of a geriatric. This one also came looking as knackered as any man would having been knocked up by our Doris at five-thirty in the morning.

He came straight over to me, and said to me, he said, 'I hear you've been having a bit of back trouble, Mr Copeland?' He spoke in that patronising manner common in doctors faced with children and anyone over the age of sixty-two, as though I wasn't just one sandwich short of a picnic, I'd left the entire basket at home.

He was also the only man who could help me right now. I said to him, I said, 'This isn't a bit of trouble, I could cope with a bit of trouble, this is excruciating.'

He hmmed as inquisitive as Zak Dingle over a pig in peril, and said to me, he said, 'I'm afraid I'll have to examine you.'

No matter how much I wanted to tell him I didn't very well expect him to read my palms, I kept my mouth shut. There's no point being mean to doctors – they're the ones with the pills. Thus, the only sounds from me were groans and, the most masculine of all sounds, the hiss – a sound that is the very essence of wincing.

Once he'd finished prodding my lower back, twisting my hips, and moving my legs as though he thought they were Play-doh, he said to me, he said, 'I think you've got a bit of lumbago, Mr Copeland.'

'Will he be able to dance?'

The doctor looked at our Doris, bewildered, and said to her, he said, 'It's recommended that he keeps regular exercise, but will be limited by his pain.'

I knew our Doris were hopeful so I said to her, I said, 'I'll give it a go, see what I can do.'

It turned out I couldn't do a lot. Despite the fact I'd been prescribed strong painkillers I could barely walk, let alone waltz.

Our Theo let me off the morning run, reluctantly. He didn't believe there was anything wrong with me – looked at me in that way mothers look at sons trying to get out of doing the dishes – but he soon realised there was something wrong when I sprawled out on the dancefloor and told him to leave me there to die.

It might have been melodramatic, but I didn't care. I kept getting these twinges that made me want to vomit more than when I got paralytic with the rugby lads in nineteen-seventy-four and they left me in a bathtub.

As if writhing on the floor in agony wasn't enough, Ken and Sheila chose to enter the ballroom. I'll be fair to Ken and admit he had the pie eyes of concern, but his Sheila looked ecstatic. Honestly. It's a wonder she didn't summon the hippos from Fantasia and dance on the ceiling, so thrilled was she at my pain.

Sheila said to me, she said, 'Having some trouble

there, Harold?'

Our Doris looked fit to murder someone. Whether me or Sheila I didn't know, but she had this look of pure fury about her – all clenched fists and hunched shoulders. She said to Sheila, she said, 'Our 'arold has had an unfortunate mishap leading to a spot of lumbago. Despite his pain he didn't want to let me down.'

She made sure to eye up Ken in that moment.

'It's a shame though. This is what, your third day of training?'

Our Theo stepped in and said, 'I'm sure your husband must have had his fair share of accidents as regional dance champion. I've no doubt you can empathise with my grandfather's brief malady.'

Sheila considered his words like a rat over a chicken leg, and said, 'Of course we empathise. Frankly it wounds me that you'd assume we'd do anything different. I suppose you're still quite young. You've a lot to learn about what not to say.'

She'd said the wrong thing.

If there's one thing our Theo hates, it's folk thinking he's incapable because of his age. He threw a copy of *Charlotte's Web* at a librarian when he was six because she said he was too young for *Animal Farm*. He never read it, but it was the principle of the thing, and our Theo gets his principles from his grandmother.

He folded his arms and gave his best Alan Sugar impression, well and truly prepared to send Sheila packing. He breathed deeply. The tension in the air was thick as custard when our Theo next spoke. He said to Sheila, he said, 'Whilst wisdom is thought to come with age and experience, you're the prime example that this clearly is far from the truth.

'I don't know the circumstances that led to you're being on this cruise. Maybe you won a competition, maybe you've more money than sense, or maybe the crew wanted someone to throw to the sharks should the boats capsize. I wouldn't wish to make assumptions because we all know to assume is to make an ass of ourselves, and I don't want to intrude on one of your favourite pastimes.

'I have known you for four days and every time I see you I throw up a little bit more in my mouth at the thought that I am unfortunate enough to share my oxygen with a woman whose only claim to fame is that she married a sofa.

'Yes Ken, I mean you. I'm not fatphobic. I'm aware of your physical achievements, but you can't deny you look like something Ikea threw out during their last sale.

'You don't need to fret about beating my grandparents anymore, because I'll be dancing with my Nan, and you'll be swept under the rug like pastry crumbs.'

All four of us looked at our Theo, astonished.

It's strange to be seeing things from the floor. From my perspective, Sheila's sneer were closer to a crevice than an expression. Her face were a right wrinkly mountain as she said to our Doris, she said, 'I can see your influence has rubbed off on your grandson, Doris. Some might say to his detriment.'

'Yes, and some might keep their mouths shut, or they'll soon experience just what it means to be a man overboard.'

'Are you threatening me?'

'I'm certainly not inviting you to watch Doctor at Sea.'

'I think we should go back to our cabin, dear,' Ken said, as meek as a mole in a fox den.

'Shut up, Ken.' This from Sheila who stared daggers at all of us. 'I don't know where you get off being such a nuisance, Doris, but you'd do well not to mess with me.'

'Did you hear her, our 'arold?' Our Doris chuckled, light and girlish. 'She calls me a nuisance. Me? I've been called worse by better people, believe me, but if I'm a nuisance I'm only following your example, Sheila.

'I refuse to get into a battle of words with you. I couldn't bear to cause you any further embarrassment. Next time we meet it will be on the dancefloor, and I sure as damn it hope they've reinforced the floorboards. I'm not sure they could cope with the weight of your ginormous ego.'

Sheila made to say something else, but Ken stopped her. He set his hands on her shoulders and led her towards the door, despite her protests. They'd be having words later, that was for sure.

I watched them leave before saying, I said, 'Now they've gone, I don't suppose you fancy helping me up?'

I spent the next few days wandering the halls of the ship with all the speed of a constipated tortoise.

Percy appointed himself my personal physiotherapist. We took up a corner of the ballroom where he talked me through stretches and light exercises in the hopes of alleviating some of my pain.

Meanwhile, our Doris and Theo trained together, glancing over every now and then when I made a particularly gruesome sound. Sometimes, it was a look of a concern, but more often than not our Doris gave me the Look, all murderous.

She wasn't happy about the situation.

In bed one evening she sat beside me and said to me, she said, 'Are you perfectly sure you won't be better for the competition, our 'arold?'

I couldn't look at her as I said, 'Not how I'm feeling, our Doris.'

'I do rather enjoy performing with our Theo, don't think otherwise, but I had grown accustomed to the idea of getting to dance with my husband.' She attempted to hide the disappointment from her voice, but it was all too present, and my heart sank like a brick through clotted cream.

'I didn't mean to get hurt.'

'I know,' she said, 'it can't be helped.'

She sighed that sigh wives have mastered over centuries to tell me that just because she understood didn't mean she wasn't upset; she emphasised the fact by switching off the bedside lamp and going silent. It took us both a while to get off to sleep, not speaking to each other, simply staring into the blue darkness of the cabin, listening to the sounds of the ship as the crew moved about the halls like Santa's elves.

Percy's exercises helped. I still had some pain, but it no longer had me wanting to fling myself into the ocean. It was less like being drilled into by a jackhammer, and more like a niggle, like someone had taken to bashing at my spine with a spatula.

Beyond Sheila and Ken, we hadn't heard of many others being interested in the competition. Yet, on the day, the halls filled with the buzz of folk all discussing their dances, and how they were looking forward to having a bit of good old-fashioned fun.

On our way to meet Theo for breakfast our Doris said to me, she said, 'I should have known there'd be others participating.'

'You didn't honestly believe it was just us, Ken and Sheila, did you? That's not much of a competition.'

'At least it means there's less of a chance of them winning.'

'You don't think you and Theo will win then?'

Our Doris did something she strove never to do, she shrugged her shoulders. Shrugging her shoulders was almost as bad as slouching in our Doris's book – I can count the amount of times our Doris has shrugged on one hand, and colour television hadn't been invented when she last did it. She said to me, she said, 'There's something particularly geriatric about dancing with your grandson. It just doesn't hold the same prestige as a married couple of more than half a century treading the boards.'

'I am sorry you know, our Doris.'

'I don't want you to be sorry, our 'arold. I want you to dance with me.'

The day passed in a haze of solemn disappointment.

Our Doris and Theo had their last training session, and whilst they were gadding about the ballroom I beggared off with Percy to the bar. I categorically refused to buy him a lime and soda and forced a pint of lager onto him. He said to me, he said, 'My body is a temple, Harry.'

I said, 'Aye, and mine's a brewery. Drink up.'

'I hope you don't mind my saying, but your head seemed to be elsewhere just now. Anything you want to talk about?'

'Our Doris wants me to dance with her tonight.'

'I know that,' he said.

'Then there's this lumbago. It's not as bad as it was, and I feel like I just might be able to dance with her, but she's more a chance of winning with our Theo.'

He glugged his lager as though he'd found an oasis in the desert before smacking his lips together and saying to me, he said, 'Sometimes, Harry, you can be a right idiot.'

I'll admit I were startled. I hadn't thought Percy the type to be so forthright and regretted not foisting lager on him sooner.

I said to him, I said, 'What do you mean?'

'Doris doesn't care about winning. She cares about showing off to the world that you two love each other enough to spend three months trapped together on this boat.'

'You have met our Doris, haven't you? She hates overt displays of affection.'

He looked wild as he clapped his hands together and exclaimed, 'That's why this is the perfect opportunity for her. It's an overt display of affection hidden beneath the guise of a dance competition. You've told me yourself that she knows everything there is to know about the social implications of holding a partner's hand in public – she'll know just what dancing tells folk, and she wants to tell folk she fancies the pants off you.'

My cheeks warmed up, more flushed than mine and our Doris's first night together, when she let me see what was really going on beneath her pinafore. I said to him, I said, 'What about Ken and Sheila?'

'This might have been about them in the beginning, but it isn't any more. She doesn't want them to win, none of us do – turns out Ken's tried this fatphobia thing with a lot of people in the hopes of guilting them out of the competition – but your wife wants to dance with you, Harry, and I recommend that no matter your pain, you choke back that ibuprofen and spend two minutes waltzing around the ballroom like she's your very own Ola Jordan.'

'I'm not too sure, Percy.'

'See how you feel after a pint,' he said, and that's the

first time I thought Percy wasn't completely off his rocker.

Frankly, I didn't believe a word Percy said. He might think our Doris wanted to share our love through the medium of dance, but he hasn't known her as long as I have and it didn't matter if she wanted to dance with me, there would be some underhanded reason behind it. I could guarantee as much.

Percy decided he needed an hour in the gym after his lager, so he left me to my own devices.

I were quite content to sit alone with my thoughts, until Veronica sauntered into the bar. She zeroed in on me, a bleeding torpedo set to obliterate me, and she didn't ask to join me, just slumped down in Percy's vacated seat, and said to me, she said, 'Your back better be on the mend, 'arold Copeland, because I can't clout a cripple.'

'Nice to see you, too, Veronica,' I said, 'maybe you'll tell me why you're after clouting me.'

'Because you're a fool.'

'Have you been speaking to Percy?'

'Yes, as it happens, but he's got nothing to do with my being here.'

'You're going to tell me that our Doris wants to dance with me and I should suck up my pain and get on with it.'

Veronica's mouth floundered, opening and closing like a goldfish with a stammer. Eventually, she found her words, saying to me, she said, 'I need a drink. Don't suppose you fancy another pint?'

'I never say no,' I said.

Once she ordered our drinks, she got straight back to the point. 'I know you must be feeling a bit delicate, but it's only a waltz. Surely you can manage that.'

'You're all acting like I made the decision not to dance with our Doris. I'm the one who told Sheila we'd be competing in the first place.' Bitter is always a good way to punctuate a sentence. I choked back a good half of my pint just to make my point.

Veronica waited until I finished. 'That might be so, but now you've got this injury. You haven't returned to see the doctor. I've checked.'

'Is there no such thing as patient confidentiality on a cruise?'

'No, there is. I happen to own the company. I only had to mention my worry that you're an insurance issue and he told me that he imagined your lumbago should have alleviated, but if you're still in pain you ought to visit him.'

'I am in pain.'

'In a few days we'll be off this ship. You'll be returning to your lives in a quaint Cheshire town and I'll be in hospital for my first dose of chemotherapy. You're behaving as though you're the first person to ever experience pain.

'I am telling you that you need to push past the pain and experience life while you still have it, 'arold.'

I stared at her for a moment, bewildered. 'I forgot,' I said, apologetic. I had. Veronica didn't hold herself as though she were ill. Of course, she had moments of still locking herself away in her cabin, but she hadn't yet missed attending the Hat Club, and when she went ashore, she always moved like a bulldozer through a bay window.

'Because I let you. I don't want folk to look at me and think that I'm just my illness, but I can't say the same for you.'

I couldn't meet her gaze, looked down at the

reflection of lights on the table.

'Are you worried about embarrassing yourself? You've nothing to worry about there – Ernest Bailey will be dancing, and he's got that inner ear thing.'

'I'm not embarrassed about dancing. I told Percy our Doris has a better chance of winning if she dances with Theo.'

'It's nothing about your lumbago then?'

'No. It is. It's just reached the point that our Theo knows the routine better than I do, and I don't want to take it away from him.'

'Doris tells me he doesn't much care for dancing with her anymore, he's only doing this as a favour to you.'

'You don't know our Theo. He's competitive. He loves his grandmother.'

'You keep telling yourself that, 'arold, but remember you have a perfectly good woman out there willing to dance with you, and at our age that's not something to be sniffed at.'

We finished our drinks and went our separate ways.

I returned to the cabin. Our Doris stood at the mirror, holding her dress against herself. It wasn't a ballgown.

I remember when she bought the dress. We were in town searching for something for the New Year's party down the Hare and Horse. Our Doris doesn't like sequins, says that although they can look attractive in the light of a disco ball, they're renowned for weighing a garment down and flying off at a moment's notice. This meant we had to find something that sparkled, that glittered, that showed the world and all its neighbours that Mrs Doris Copeland of Shakespeare Avenue knew a thing or two about making a fashion statement.

We spent weeks looking for something. We tried Bon Marche, Marks and Spencer, BHS, we even tried Fat Face when our Doris thought she saw something in their top window, only to discover it was a Christmas bauble. There'd been a dress at John Lewis, but she felt theirs was a national name and as such available to too many women to be truly individual.

When she had me walk down the main arcade for what felt like the fifty-thousandth time I reached the end of my tether. In fact, there was no tether left. The tether was well and truly lost, and I were straggling along after our Doris in a state of desperation. I said to her, I practically yelled – I spoke as loud as our Doris will allow me in a public place – saying, I said, 'For crying out loud, our Doris, we've been walking all day, is it so important to wear a dress everyone will be too drunk to remember by morning?'

She'd been about to give me the Look, eyes set to be piercing, lips about to purse when she saw the dress.

Everything stopped.

She stood stock still in the middle of the street staring at the boutique window in awe. A mannequin in a purple rhinestone dress, looking every inch the Doctor Who villain, stood beneath an assortment of fairy lights.

Our Doris had found her dress.

Now she stood holding it against her body, no trace of happiness left.

I said to her, I said, 'Are you all right, our Doris?'

'I'm fine, our 'arold, just thinking about how I best go and get ready.' She hung the dress on the wardrobe door and disappeared into the en-suite.

I settled down on the edge of the bed. Sometimes it doesn't do for a seventy-six-year-old man to feel sorry for himself, but after words from Percy and Veronica, and seeing our Doris so despondent, I felt I could do anything but.

Dinner that evening was a strange affair. Our shipmates were ecstatic at this being our last night at sea. They chattered like geese over a loaf of bread, sharing complimentary champagne and admiring one another's dance costumes. Meanwhile, our Doris spent most of the evening staring at her food as though it were an enigma to her.

At least our Theo were happy at getting to wear his suit.

Soon enough it was time for the dance competition.

The crew had been hard at work to make the ballroom spectacular. Round tables surrounded the dancefloor, draped in white tablecloths, steam-pressed, and not a corner out of place.

Our judges were already situated. Five of our fellow travellers who had no interest in competing, and some minor knowledge of dance they'd gleaned from Strictly Come Dancing and YouTube tutorials, sat at the edge of the dancefloor. They were dressed to impress, suited and booted to the nines. It was a row of tuxedoes and ballgowns – elegance personified, and mildly intimidating.

On the end of their table, stood the trophy. It really did look as though it had been bought from a market stall in Bangkok. It was as tacky as a Christmas ornament, in the shape of a geisha girl balancing a koi carp on her shoulder. No matter what it looked like, I knew our Doris wanted to possess it.

She was impressed, eyeing up everything. We walked

arm in arm as Theo led the way to a table.

He'd clearly been following instructions because he chose a table not too far away from the dancefloor that we can't see what's going on, but not too close that people may think we're too eager.

We were joined by Veronica and Percy. He had no interest in competing, choosing to abstain because although he attends regular Zumba classes, he hasn't the first idea about dance. He also didn't have a partner, but I thought it cruel to point that out.

'Are you ready for your dance then, Doris?' Veronica asked, a slight slur to her speech that spoke of one too many tequila sunrises with dinner.

Our Doris summoned her public smile and said to her, she said, 'I am. It's been so long since Theo and I last danced that I can't help but be most enthusiastic at the prospect.'

'How wonderful.' Veronica made sure to send a wink my way.

To make matters worse Ken and Sheila came lumbering towards our table like the rejects from Fraggle Rock. Ken's face gleamed with sweat. His cheeks were as red as old chorizo and we hadn't even danced. He wore a dress suit that strained to stay shut, whilst the top button of his shirt looked to be cutting off his circulation.

Sheila wore yellow.

Bright yellow.

As yellow as a canary, or a dandelion. Her ever-present sneer was enhanced by proper red lipstick. She'd gone for the femme fatale and ended up looking like a well-dressed corpse.

Despite our months in some of the world's hottest countries she was pale, and gaunt. She'd had a bash at contouring her cheekbones only to leave herself with deep hollows, great skeletal caverns where she'd hoped for definition.

Our Doris said to her, she said, 'I see someone's been playing at dress up.'

'I knew you'd have something to say. I told Ken you'd have something to say.'

'I always have something to say, Sheila. Sometimes I have to consider what I can utter in the company of others.'

'It doesn't matter anyway. You've no idea the look I'm going for to complement our routine.'

'If you're going for a vampiric take on Ursula Andress I'd say you're spot on,' I said.

Ken chipped in saying, he said, 'I really don't think you should be saying things like that to Sheila. It's uncalled for.'

'She tell you to say that, did she?'

He stammered, caught between the need to breathe and the need to defend himself, giving him the look of someone with a significant bladder urgency.

'You've room to talk,' Sheila interjected, 'Doris has you so securely under her thumb you're no more a man than a fingerprint.'

'On the contrary, Sheila. Mine and 'arold's marriage is a partnership cultivated over fifty-six years. The best you can hope for is three months down the pie shop.'

'In that case I feel sorry for you, Harold. Fifty-six years spent with a woman who makes enemies wherever she goes.'

'You think highly of yourself,' our Doris said, 'I haven't known you long enough to call you an enemy. Quite honestly you're nothing more than a pain in the neck.'

'Aye,' I said, 'easily fixed with a bit of hydrotherapy.'

Me and our Doris looked at each other and set about laughing. She didn't use her polite titter either, she gave me her bawdy, full-blown laugh.

'You can't be saying things like that, our 'arold. Suppose Sheila were to think it a threat.'

'Don't be funny, our Doris. I don't for a moment think she has enough capacity for thoughts like that.'

Sheila and Ken had no idea what we were talking about. They stood there, completely oblivious to the fact they were being insulted.

Even the others were struggling. They exchanged glances but they'd never get it so there was no point explaining. Sometimes, there are things only a husband and wife can understand.

Sheila gathered herself together and made her parting shot, she said, 'At least my husband isn't too embarrassed to dance with me, but then my scalp doesn't look like the wrong end of a turnip.'

Our Doris stared at her, she didn't bother with the Look, her face fell slightly, lip attempted a tremble before she said to Sheila, she said, 'What a wonderful observation you've made, Sheila. Did it take you the whole of three months to come up with it, or did you make use of the WiFi and get the internet to do what your brain could not?'

Sheila didn't respond. She and Ken went to find a table, leaving us to feel the weight of her words.

I was going to console our Doris, set my hand on her shoulder and reiterate that I was suffering but I was too late.

The lights went low. Music blared from the speakers, and Betty Fiddles entered the ballroom. They must have been six-foot-tall without heels.

Betty was a vision in gold. Sequins and rhinestones galore covered every inch of her dress, giving her the appearance of a trophy. Her hair was a cloud of blonde waves piled like dusky mashed potato.

Her face were that heavily caked with make up she could've been a plasterer in a previous life.

And she was entertaining. She had jokes and one-liners and music, like the variety acts of old. I found myself reminded of Les Dawson, only in a ballgown with six-inch stilettos.

Too soon the act was over, and time came for the competition. Betty stayed on to introduce the first act to the floor.

Gareth and Julie McCrimmon were a shy pair as they scuttled about the place, not so much dancing as stepping out of rhythm. I forgave them their nerves, but Gareth spent the entire time holding Julie at arm's length, as though he'd never touched a girl before.

Some of the other couples weren't much better. Gina Stourbridge tripped over her dress knocking her David to the ground. He bashed his knee and said as he knew he never should have danced with a woman who thought the paso doble were an Italian cheese dish.

They didn't score well.

There were some standouts. Michael and Chris Boothroyd performed a lift that was equal parts impressive and terrifying, none more so because they danced to The Logic Song. Callum and Ruth Leadbetter spun that much I were in danger of getting vertigo. And the Marsdens shocked us all with their routine to Hungry Eyes.

Eventually, Ken and Sheila took to the dancefloor. He loosened his top button as they stepped into the spotlight, centre stage.

They danced.

My stomach gurgled like a blocked washing machine because Ken was good.

The routine brought back memories of Natasha Kaplinsky on Strictly. They exuded confidence, and for all his faults Ken knew how to lead.

The pair of them made full use of the floor. They had spins and dips and lifts, choreographed to a tee, professional, and I were jealous. I were seething.

Sure, Ken was sweating more than a sumo wrestler in a sauna, but he had this grace about him as he did it.

Sheila followed him, ever aware of the grand spectacle they made. I still don't know what story she wished to tell with her make-up because it had nothing to do with an Argentine Tango to Lady Gaga.

When they finished, they bowed. No one else bowed. But then no one else received a standing ovation.

Sheila stared at us, all smug as she resumed her seat.

Betty Fiddles announced an interval and I was one of the first to flee the ballroom, leaving everyone else behind.

Our Theo caught up with me in the hall. 'Grandad,' he said, 'are you all right?'

I slouched against a wall. I couldn't find the words. There were a lump in my throat as heavy as Kilimanjaro and it wouldn't budge.

Our Theo leant against the wall beside me and said, he said, 'I imagine I'm too sick to dance with Nan. Don't suppose you could help me out and step in?'

I was astounded.

I was baffled.

I was every single synonym of shocked there is to be had. I looked at our Theo, not quite believing his words and said to him, I said, 'Are you sure?'

'You should dance with Nan. She's all right dancing with me, but I'm not her husband.'

The matter was settled.

I couldn't say no.

I were set to accept our Theo's offer when I realised who stood behind him, the fury of seven Gordon Ramsey's bubbling in her veins.

She gave me the most vicious Look she had ever given me in fifty-six years, worse than when I hoovered up the hamster, even worse than when I'd been seen in the same cloakroom as Eleanor Stockwell.

She practically bellowed at me, saying, she said, 'Who do you think you are to leave me sat there like that, 'arold Copeland?'

'Nan, he were just –'

'Don't defend him, Theo.' She glowered at me. I felt smaller than the smallest amoeba. Richard Hammond under a microscope. 'Sheila and Ken just proved their worth as dancers. We will have to eat our words. Rather than stay and console me, you beggar off with no more than a kiss my backside nor nothing.'

A sharp intake from our Theo who'd never heard his grandmother speak so crudely in public.

I said to her, I said, 'I left because I can only disappoint you, our Doris.'

She glanced over at our Theo and told him, as politely as she could, to push off.

He scarpered, leaving the two of us facing each other in the hall. I didn't know if this were going Gunfight at the OK Corral, or Sleepless in Seattle, but I were nervous.

Our Doris got herself together and tried to reduce the Look to a simmer. She said, 'You've already disappointed me, our 'arold.' I made to speak, but she stopped me. 'I don't deny you've been in pain, but when I realised you wouldn't dance with me, I didn't see the point in continuing. Our Theo can tell my heart's not in it.

'I know we set out to beat Ken and Sheila, and since there's no chance of that happening now, I don't mind saying this: when I thought we were going to dance together again, I felt like I had something to look forward to for the first time in a long while. It also meant us getting to show everyone what we mean to each other, because despite the fact you read the Daily Mirror, have a misogynistic interest in female gardening personalities of the nineteen-nineties, and never put your dentures away properly, you mean the world to me, our 'arold, and I wanted to make sure you knew it.'

Apparently, grown men don't just cry at lumbago and football, because listening to our Doris's words had tears catching at my eyes. They could have been emotional, or the glare from our Doris's dress, either way she leant me her handkerchief.

I said to her, I said, 'I thought you didn't go in for overt displays of affection, our Doris.'

She found a smile and said, 'I shouldn't get used to it, our 'arold, it'll be a side effect of the sea air.'

I said, feeling just like I did when I asked her out to the pictures for the first time, I said, 'Will you dance with me, our Doris?'

'I'll have to check my dance card.'

We returned to the ballroom as the second half began. We barely had time to sit down when Betty Fiddles called out our names.

My heartbeat thrummed against my ear drums. There were a few twinges in my back but that was nothing compared to the headache building behind my eyes, as though preparing to pop from my skull like little ocular marbles.

I led our Doris around the dancefloor as Elvis got on with his crooning.

I kept my eyes on hers as the entire time, trapped in her Medusa-strength stare. I've called our Doris in the past, but she does have something alluring in her irises; just one look and I'm ensnared like an insect in a Venus Flytrap.

We strayed from our Theo's routine a few times. After a few rotations, I grew bored of the same old same old. That's the problem with the waltz, no variation, at least not the way we do it. Sometimes I dipped our Doris despite there being no occasion to dip or spun her towards Ken and Sheila's table so she could grin at them.

My spine protested, my legs did their own thing, but I found I couldn't help grinning like a daft 'un as our song came to a close.

We were met with applause. Our Doris took my hand and had me bow to them as she curtsied a curtsey as regal as Buckingham Palace.

We returned to our table to the wide grins of Theo, Veronica and Percy.

'You were brilliant,' Theo said, springing from his chair.

Our Doris said, 'Thank you, Theo. Although you'll note that some of your grandfather's moves weren't really in keeping with a waltz.'

'You loved every minute of it,' said Veronica, 'you look as bonny as a schoolgirl.'

We didn't pay much attention to those who danced after us. Veronica ordered a round and we sat talking about our plans when we got home. Our Doris talked about seeing our Angela, and Erin, and Edith and Alf – she planned an itinerary of friends she must visit in our first days back. Personally, I were harbouring thoughts about my geraniums, but I wasn't going to let on to our Doris.

Percy planned to go straight into training for the London Marathon. He said to me, he said, 'You could come down and train with me, Harry. Make sure you stay in shape so your back doesn't go out again.'

'A bit of a jog round the ship had me flagging. Twenty-six miles would see me in a coffin.'

'And just where do you train, Percy?' asked our Doris, a twinkle in her eye, all mischievous, and even though I knew it wouldn't last I were glad of it.

After an age, they finally decided to announce the winner of the dance competition.

Betty Fiddles had touched up her make-up and

readjusted her wig for the occasion. She took a piece of paper from the head judge and said the words we knew she'd say, 'The winners are Ken and Sheila Owen.'

Sheila attempted to appear shocked but looked more like Uncle Fester post-electrocution. The two of them wandered over to Betty, who had a conciliatory expression on her face. Well, as close as she could get to consoling with three lots of fake eyelashes stacked on top of one another. She said to the pair of them, she said, 'Ordinarily at this moment I would be awarding you a trophy, but earlier this evening it went missing and the crew have been unable to locate it. Therefore, it is my pleasure to present you with two complimentary glasses of Cava courtesy of Mrs Veronica Ambrose.'

Ken accepted his glass gallantly.

The same couldn't be said for Sheila.

She spun and faced us, her heels squealing like a crushed cockroach on the floorboards. Her eyes were as maniacal as Cruella de Vil after the dalmatians. 'You!' she exclaimed, storming over in a huff. A huff that was somewhat dampened by the drunken stagger to her gait.

Ken made to stop Sheila, but Betty held him back. She sipped from Sheila's glass as intent on seeing this drama play out as any man who'd spent six hours in heels.

Everyone watched. Cyril Marsden turned to his good ear – he wouldn't be able to see what was going on, but he'd sure as heck know what was being said.

Our Doris stood up to meet Sheila. She'd composed her face into something I recognised as being absolutely terrifying. It's an expression that gives away nothing, all stoic, as though she could be about to assassinate you and you wouldn't realise until the chorus of ashes to ashes.

Sheila said to her, she said, 'I know you're jealous of me and Ken, but this takes the cake. We won, Doris. You didn't. We're better than you. Get over it and give us back the trophy.'

Our Doris surveyed the entirety of the ballroom, centred her gaze on Sheila and said to her, she said, 'I must say you did a particularly spectacular job tonight, Sheila. I found myself suitably impressed by your routine and understand just why Ken is regional champion. Seeing a semi-professional dancer win is most heartening for all us amateurs. Now, I'm afraid I don't know anything about a trophy being stolen, but believe me, if it were in my possession, I would love nothing more than to award it to you.'

Sheila were flabbergasted. Our Doris had caught her on the wrong foot. She said to her, she said, 'Even if Ken wasn't a dancer, he'd still run rings around the lot of you.'

'I've no doubt about it. It's one of the reasons I'm dismayed not to get the opportunity to give you your trophy. A few clouts would be more than enough to fix the issue with that big head of yours.'

This had Sheila laughing. She said to our Doris, she said, 'You think you're smart, don't you, but you've just threatened me in front of witnesses. I'll have you for that.'

Our Doris breathed deep, inhaling through her nose, exhaling through the mouth like some sort of Tibetan monk. 'Sadly, this isn't an episode of Emmerdale, and I'm well aware I cannot get away with any form of physical violence. Whilst it may have seemed like a threat, that was not my intention. I simply wished to express the idea that I have grown quite tired of your arrogance, and this idea that every movement I make is meant to hurt you in some way.

'I don't care, Sheila. I came on this cruise to see the world with my husband, find some enjoyment in new, exotic places, and simply relax. I hope you haven't missed out on the same by being so increasingly obsessed with my actions.'

Our Doris picked her glass up off the table. She spoke to everyone when next she spoke, saying, she said, 'Since it looks like they won't get their trophy, I say we raise a toast to Sheila and Ken, a couple who so desperately need it. To Sheila and Ken!'

There was a dull chorus as their names were repeated, like the drone of a beehive threatening a nursery.

Our Doris sipped her drink and offered Sheila a smile. 'Good luck to you, Sheila, I hope our paths never cross again.'

Sheila, defeated, headed back to Ken and they returned to their seats.

Betty Fiddles blinked a few times, disappointment etched into every single bone in her body. She'd expected drama, to see Sheila tear the headscarf from our Doris's head and use it as a noose. Instead, she'd got polite anger and a toast.

She brought the microphone up again and said, she said, 'Well wasn't that just lovely. I'd have toasted the couple myself but apparently I've no need to. There's going to be a bit of music in here, if you fancy sticking around for a boogie.

'Anyway, I'm off for a lie down. Is there a gentleman out there who'd like to escort me back to my cabin?'

We applauded Betty as she switched off the microphone and disappeared out into the hall. A few moments later, Percy proclaimed he was off to see a man about a horse. He gave us a wink and followed her out.

'I hope he knows what he's getting himself into,' I said.

Our Doris shook her head and said to me, she said, 'Sometimes, our 'arold, you can be completely oblivious to what's right under your nose.'

'She's right, Grandad.' Our Theo stood up as music filled the ballroom once more. 'Are you two staying for a dance?'

I said to our Doris, I said, 'What do you think?'

She did something I never expected her to do, but I suppose we were on a ship in the middle of the ocean, with no way of it getting back to anyone in Partridge Mews. Our Doris kissed me, and this weren't a peck on the cheek either, this were a lipstick smearing, lip smacking kiss. It tasted of fifty-six years, and half a bottle of champagne.

When it was over, I blinked. I were shell-shocked. I said to her, I said, 'Is that a yes, then, our Doris?'

We danced. Of course, we did. I got some points off our Theo for showing the world what proper Grandad dancing looks like – all shuffles and a recreation of the twist that looked more like a fight with incontinence. Meanwhile, he danced with Veronica and our Doris, getting to perform the routine he'd missed.

We carried on well into the night, all of us aware that this was our last night of frivolity before we returned to civilisation. We'd been three months away from Partridge Mews, and I couldn't help but wonder just what our Doris would be like when we got home, but that was a thought for another day. I pushed it aside and danced as though I didn't have lumbago, I wasn't anywhere near as suave as Fred Astaire, but I did a good impression.

All too soon, the music stopped.

We left Veronica to her own devices and walked our Theo back to his room. Not because he needed a chaperone, just so our Doris could make sure he had packed to a standard required from a grandson of a middle-class retiree from Cheshire.

'I'm glad you two could work things out,' he said. He hugged us both, before closing the door.

As we walked back to our cabin, I said to our Doris, I said, 'I'm glad we worked things out as well.'

She gave me the Look, well as much of a look as she could muster with a smile on her face, and said, 'If you hadn't called Ken fat this never would have happened, our 'arold.'

'Aren't you glad I insult folk then?'

'I suppose it makes a change.'

We hadn't been back in our cabin two minutes when there was a knock at the door. Our Doris had been in the process of removing her headscarf. Her hair doesn't look too bad now. Sure, there are still some awkward lengths and tufts, but she's taken full advantage of the ships' salon. Although she hasn't got a full-blown perm, there are some small curls bouncing on her head, like a fresh-groomed cockerpoo. Either way, she took one look at herself in the mirror before saying, 'Beggar it,' and opening the door.

Veronica hurried into the room with a pile of fabric in her arms. She'd concealed something inside its folds.

Our Doris said to her, she said, 'Veronica, you didn't?'

'I did.'

'What? What's she done?' I said.

She let the fabric spill to the floor, and everything became clear. 'It's amazing what you can hide in a size twenty-four kaftan from Bon Marche.'

I couldn't believe my eyes. 'You stole the trophy?'

'I couldn't bear the idea of it going to that Sheila. Sure, Ken's an all right fella when he's on his own at the buffet, but she is something else.'

'We know that, Veronica, but is that really a reason to steal the trophy?'

Veronica shrugged and handed it to our Doris. 'My ship, my rules.'

The trophy reflected in our Doris's eyes. She were enamoured, trapped in the allure of gold paint. She said to Veronica, she said, 'It's kind of you to think of us, but this isn't right. It should go to Ken and Sheila.'

'You might not have been the best dancers tonight, but you're the more deserving. Shove this in your bag and we'll say no more about it.' She pulled our Doris into her arms, squeezing her that tight I thought our Doris's head might pop off. 'I've really enjoyed getting to know you, Doris. You're not everyone's cup of tea, but you're all right in my book.'

She didn't say anything to me as she left, speeding out as fast as she'd entered.

I said to our Doris, I said, 'Well I'm baffled.'

She looked from the door to me to and said, 'I needed this, our 'arold.'

'I know you did, love,' I said, and I wasn't just talking about the trophy.

Acknowledgements

I didn't anticipate Doris Ahoy being its own book, but the story grew more than I thought possible.

A few people have helped me along the way.

Firstly, Lindsey Watson has been by my side since I began my writing journey. You have proven to be one of the most supportive friends a person could ask for, and I am eternally grateful.

Cathryn Heathcote read this book before anyone else and was kind enough not to mention the typos immediately.

Thanks are also due to Joy Winkler, Abercrombie, Ste and Margaret Holbrook, Sandy Milsom, Phil Poyser, Jason Sandywell and the Macclesfield Creative Writing Group for continuing to support my work.

I would like to express my gratitude to the many Booktubers who have read and reviewed my books over the last few years. You have helped introduce our Doris to readers all over the world and this has warmed my heart on many an occasion.

For those of you have been here since the beginning, until next time, that is all.

45962543R00092

Printed in Poland
by Amazon Fulfillment
Poland Sp. z o.o., Wrocław